WISH TO BE LIKE YOU

LOVE'S AWAKENING

MOHIT GHANSELA

Contents

Acknowledgments

I would like to extend my special thanks to my friends, who played a crucial role in introducing me to the captivating stories that have influenced this novel. I am immensely grateful to Muskan for being a true source of inspiration, igniting my passion for writing. I also want to express my heartfelt gratitude to Agreema for patiently listening to my tales and providing unwavering support throughout this creative journey. It is through their encouragement that this novel has become a reality. Thank you, Agreema and Muskan, for your invaluable contributions.

1

Caught in Her Gaze

As per the report of the National Science Foundation, it was found that the average person has about 12,000 to 60,000 thoughts per day, of which 80% of thoughts are negative. "What nonsense!!!" I suddenly heard a voice behind me. As I turned to face the source of the voice, I saw her for the first time. She was a girl with brown hair and sharp eyes, her forehead glistening with sweat, and her shoes caked in dirt as though she had been playing before shouting out to her group. Curiously, I asked my friend Shantanu who she was. He spoke without any change in his posture, delivering a stinging response with a sharp edge in his voice, "Am I expected to possess such knowledge?" "His words stung, and I felt a twinge of frustration." But then, almost as an afterthought, he added, "Why don't you go and ask her yourself?"

Shantanu was my closest confidante, the only person I trusted enough to share my ATM pin code too. But this time following his advice carried more weight than just that. As I looked around, I couldn't find the girl anywhere. "Did you happen to see where she went?" I asked Shantanu, my voice tinged with urgency.

Shantanu warned me not to disturb him since he wasn't in a good mood. But I couldn't resist my curiosity and asked him once again, "Bro, did you see where she went?" I nudged his shoulder and urged him to speak up. However, the sudden transformation of Shantanu caught me off guard. He went from his usual calm demeanor to a scowl so fierce that it sent shivers down my spine. It was like he had turned into Terence, a character from Angry Birds, ready to unleash his wrath on anything in his path.

I closed my eyes in fear, unsure of what to do next. Suddenly, a single note of music played in my eardrums for what felt like an eternity, Shantanu left the ground and before leaving the ground, he said, "Yes," I saw her. I felt a pang of disappointment mixed with a tinge of anger. How could he be so dismissive and rude? I turned my face away, pretending to be interested in something else.

"With a heavy heart, I headed back home. The walk felt longer than usual. "Just for a look," I thought, "it was more than I paid today." With this thought in mind, I entered my house.

As soon as I entered, my mom greeted me, "You 're home. Go wash your hands before I bring the food up."

I replied, "I am already full, Mom," although I thought to myself, "Yeah, why not?"

Don't make a fool of me, okay?" she retorted, her eyes narrowing. This is your favorite dish, 'rajma chawal' (a popular North Indian dish made with red kidney beans cooked in a spicy tomato-based gravy and served with steamed rice), and I specially cooked it for you."

I responded with an unpleasant tone, "So what? I said I am full. Why are you not understanding?"

This is common with us whenever we are in a bad mood or unhappy. We are not only ruining our day, but we are also becoming the reason for someone's bad day too.

But, as a mother and a true friend of mine, she could sense that something was bothering me. She gently asked me if I had fought in school or if someone was bullying me. I hesitated at first, not wanting to share the real reason for fear of getting scolded. But my mom assured me that she would not share it with anyone and encouraged me to open up.

I finally mustered the courage to tell her that Shantanu had slapped me today. My mom's initial reaction surprised me as she chuckled and found it funny. She asked me why Shantanu had slapped me, I hesitated and thought to myself that if I told her the truth, I might get into more trouble. So, I lied to her and said that I had advised Shantanu to concentrate on his studies and not to waste time with girls.

My mom's concern immediately kicked in, and she reassured me that there was nothing wrong with what I had said. She even offered to talk to Shantanu's mother about his behavior. However, I tried to downplay the situation and told her it wasn't necessary since Shantanu was not her son, but I was. I then used my innocent charm to ask her to bring me some rajma chawal since I was feeling hungry.

"My mom, being the insightful woman she is, didn't let me off the hook so easily. She insisted that I apologize first for my behavior and have my meal by myself. I complied, realizing that my mom was not only a caring parent but also a responsible friend who taught me important values of accountability, owning up to my actions, and treating others with respect."

This is the way she teaches me in my life. As a friend, she pampers me and upbringing me as a mother.

After getting smacked by my buddy and telling a fib to my Mom, I sat in my room and started thinking about the girl who cut me off while I was talking today.

And then I remembered Mark Zuckerberg's words,

"Mark Zuckerberg once said, 'Facebook's mission is to give people the power to build community and bring the world closer together,' and I've decided to contribute to his mission. So now, I'm on a mission of my own.

Technology has made our lives easier than ever before, but it's still useless if you don't know the right lyrics of the song or the name of the person you're searching for. For instance, just today, I tried to search for the 'brown hair girl I saw on the school ground,' but alas, no results were found."

After tirelessly scouring the app for what felt like hours, I was at my wit's end. No matter how hard I tried, I just couldn't seem to find the right result. Frustration consumed me, and I blurt out, "What the heck? I mean, I've searched high and low, left and right, and still, I can't find what I'm looking for. Mark, what's going on with your app?"

"Hey Mark, your application doesn't really bring me closer to the world, but I did stumble upon a guy named Ankit with a profile picture that looked like Salman Khan. At first, I was like, 'Wait, did Salman Khan change his name to Ankit or something?' But after scrolling down, I found multiple profiles with Salman Khan's face but different names. It was pretty confusing, to be honest."

"I started to think again, 'Hey Mark, is this really how you're bringing the world closer to us?' In your world, all I find are Salman Khans and no brown-haired girl whom I saw today. Your application seems pretty useless to me. After saying all this, I decided to call it quits and not participate in his mission anymore.

At around 6 PM in the evening, I heard someone calling my name from downstairs and knocking on the door repeatedly. To my dismay, I realized that it was Shantanu, the guy who had slapped me earlier. I tried to stop my mother from letting him in, but unfortunately, she had already opened the door and was inquiring about the incident. After taking a few moments to understand the situation, Shantanu apologized for what he had done. Despite what had happened, I couldn't help but feel sorry for him. Once he was allowed entry, he made his way into my room

As I looked at Shantanu, I could feel the tension in the air. He spoke, "So I was looking for the girl, aha...and you were there to correct me," with a smirk on his face.

I smiled back, happy to finally be in the right. "Yes," I replied, enjoying the moment.

Shantanu rolled his eyes. "Oh! Brainless person, the day when I take your advice is the last day of my life."

I couldn't help but laugh. "Oh, really? Please let me know before going on that journey. I will celebrate with pastries and cheeseburgers."

Shantanu shook his head, still smiling. "Yeah, sure."

But I didn't want to beat around the bush any longer. "So, what do you want? An apology?"

Shantanu's smile faded, and he looked down. "I'm sorry for what I did. I was upset, and your constant questioning only added to my frustration," he said in a remorseful tone.

Shantanu and I became friends in the second grade after participating in an activity on sharing and caring, which was led by our favorite teacher, Ms. Poonam. During the activity, we discovered that we both had matching lunch boxes adorned with identical Bob the Builder stickers. This shared interest allowed us to connect and I was able to share my food with Shantanu for the first time. This experience opened the door to a friendship with Shantanu, who became an important presence in my life.

As Shantanu tapped his fingers on the table, and asked, "Hey, what are you thinking now? Ask me at least why I was upset. I am here to share with you!"

With a playful smile, I replied, "Will you teach me how to use Facebook if I listen to your problem?"

"As I looked into Shantanu's eyes, I sensed a deep unease in his demeanor. It was as though something was weighing heavily on his mind, something he couldn't bring himself to express. He took a step back, his hand reaching for the door handle. But I knew I couldn't let him leave without getting to the bottom of his troubles.

"Hey, wait," I said, my voice gentle and reassuring. "I'm sorry if I came across as flippant before. I didn't mean to belittle your problems. Please, stay a little longer and talk to me. I'm here to listen and help in any way I can."

Shantanu hesitated, his hand still on the door handle. But then, with a sigh, he turned back towards me. "It's just... I've been feeling really lost lately," he said, his voice heavy with emotion. "Like I don't know where my life is headed or what I'm supposed to be doing. It's been eating away at me for weeks now, and I don't know what to do about it."

I nodded sympathetically, understanding all too well the feeling of being adrift in life. Shantanu revealed that his mother had been diagnosed with liver failure, and his father was due to be transferred to Hyderabad the following month. He was struggling to figure out how to manage these challenges, and it was clear that they were weighing heavily on his mind. Then, he started crying."

At that moment, I realized the true depth of our friendship. It wasn't just about the good times and laughter we shared. It was about being there for each other in the tough moments too. It was about being a shoulder to cry on when things got overwhelming. And even though I wasn't sure what to say to comfort my friend, I knew that my presence alone meant something to him.

After a few minutes, we both calmed down and sat on the couch. Shantanu opened up more about his struggles and we talked about possible solutions. We brainstormed together and came up with some ideas on how to manage the challenges he was facing. By the end of our conversation, we both felt a sense of relief and hope.

It was the first time in 10 years of our friendship that we had a sentimental talk, and it felt good to connect on a deeper level.

After some time, Shantanu shared that he felt better and even revealed the name of the girl I had seen earlier on the school ground as Aadhya.

However, when I asked him how he knew her, he became evasive and refused to answer my questions. I persisted, hoping to learn more, but he told me that he had to go now and promised to tell me more about her tomorrow.

This is the only bad habit he had, he yearned for anyone by switching off the conversation in the middle.

A minute later, my mom arrived and asked if I had resolved the issues with Shantanu after our fight. At first, I was confused, but then I remembered the lie I had told her. I said that Shantanu had come to apologize, and I had forgiven him. My mom laughed, and it seemed like she knew the truth behind my lie. But I still elaborated on my story, explaining that Shantanu had apologized and cried, and since he didn't have any other friends, he had to come to me.

My mom then gave me some advice, saying that whenever I feel like I am the only one for someone, it's my responsibility to never let them down. At the time, I didn't fully understand what she meant or maybe I wasn't interested in her words since I was only 17. But looking back, I realize the wisdom in her advice and how it applies to all types of relationships.

Assembly time

The morning assembly began with the sound of drums echoing through the school grounds. The students were excitedly sorted into their classes and sections, eager to start their day.

After the prayer and singing of the national anthem, Mrs. Sarojini Basu, the principal, stepped up to give her speech. She started her address with a loud and patriotic "Bharat Mata ki jai."

As the speech began, I started searching for Aadhya in the crowd. But our math teacher, Mr. Kapil Malhotra, warned me to pay attention and not look around. Ignoring his warning, I continued scanning the crowd.

Suddenly, Mr. Malhotra appeared by my side and caught my ear, leading me out of the assembly for not paying attention. When I stepped out, I found Aadhya standing right in front of me, laughing and making funny faces. I felt embarrassed and wished I had listened to Mr. Malhotra's warning.

To add to my embarrassment, the principal announced Aadhya's name for an award. Mr. Malhotra mocked me for my mistake, saying "Hey shameless, clap now." I felt even more foolish as I was the only one clapping in the wrong direction.

"So, I came to know that Aadhya won the award for a debate competition she participated in a week before, at St. Thomas school, which involved 12 other schools."

After the morning assembly ended, I made my way toward my classroom when one of my classmates, Rajat, approached me with a curious expression. He asked me which school I had attended before coming to this one.

I decided to attend this new school because of its proximity to my house and the fact that my best friend Shantanu was already a student there, though in a different section. It has only been 10 days since I started at this school, and while I am not yet familiar with many of the students, I already sense that this school is different from the others I've attended in the past.

Rajat asked me where I had been and which school I attended before. I replied that I had attended Bluebells. He smiled and left to join his group. Rajat's smile indicated that he was asking the question to tease or mock me, rather than out of genuine interest.

"After entering my classroom, I discovered that summer vacation was just five days away and that my syllabus was incomplete." To try to finish my syllabus before the vacation began, I started borrowing notebooks from my classmates." However, it was challenging as I did not have any friends in the class, and everyone was refusing to lend me their notebooks by giving excuses.

Luckily, among them, there was one girl named Anamika, who showed empathy toward me. She kindly said, "Take this, but give it back before the summer vacation." Her generosity was a relief to me, and I felt grateful for her help.

While everyone was eagerly anticipating the upcoming summer vacation, I was worried about how I would be able to complete the syllabus in my notebook in just five days. I confided in Anamika about my concerns, and she offered to assist me by explaining some of the topics to me.

However, as she lent me her notebook, she also asked for my number and said, "I'll call you when I need my notebook back, and you'll have to come and return it." It was a reasonable request, and I agreed without hesitation.

As I sat and relaxed in the classroom, my mind drifted back to that morning's assembly where Aadhya had tried to provoke me. I tried to let go of my frustration and instead focused on the present moment. However, my attention was soon diverted when Aadhya walked into the classroom.

"Attention, everyone!" she exclaimed. "Our classes will be merged for the next five days."

I could feel the energy in the room shift as everyone processed this unexpected news. But instead of paying attention to what Aadhya was saying, my eyes were drawn to her hair, which was now black, a stark contrast to the brown locks I had seen her sporting just a few days ago.

I wondered what had prompted such a sudden change. Was it a new look she was trying out, or was there something more mysterious at play? I couldn't shake off the thought that maybe she was a vampire, even though it seemed like a ridiculous notion.

As Aadhya continued to speak, I found myself lost in my thoughts, pondering the possibilities. Her brown eyes seemed to shine brighter than usual, adding to the mystery surrounding her. I knew that I was being ridiculous, but the thought of Aadhya being a vampire was too tantalizing to let go.

I shook my head, trying to clear my mind of these silly notions. (*Shifting the section*)

As I entered the classroom, I looked around and searched for my friend, Shantanu. There he was, hunched over some math problems. I called out to him, hoping he would be able to spare a few minutes to talk.

"Hey, Shantanu!" I said, trying to get his attention.

"Not now, I have to complete my coaching work," he replied, not even looking up from his notebook.

I persisted, "When did you start your coaching? You didn't tell me."

Shantanu's response was dripping with sarcasm, "You should know this, and what did you do this morning? Listen, Atharv, this is class 11. Be serious in your life."

I hung my head in shame and muttered, "Okay," and started to work on the missed syllabus.

As I worked, Shantanu continued to scribble notes in his notebook, muttering to himself about the sandwich theorem. Curious, I asked, "What's that all about?"

Shantanu replied, "Be quiet for a while."

Feeling bored and restless, I tried to start a conversation. "I'm feeling bored," I told him.

Shantanu put down his pen and looked at me. "Use this free time. Why don't you try some molarity and molality questions?" he suggested.

I laughed and replied, "Chemistry is easy, bro."

Shantanu retorted with a hint of sarcasm, "Haha... yeah, still four subjects left."

I then reminded him, "You promised to tell me about Aadhya."

But Shantanu was too engrossed in his work to care. "Will you please keep quiet? This question is so confusing. Let me concentrate," he snapped.

I gazed up at Shantanu with my best puppy-dog eyes and asked innocently, "What is her full name? Does she have an account on Facebook?"

Shantanu's expression suddenly shifted with frustration. He rose from his seat and requested, "Aadhya, could you please come here for a minute?" His tone was firm yet calm, but his vexation was still palpable. I could sense his annoyance, and I felt a pang of regret for pushing the subject.

As Shantanu called out to Aadhya, my heart began to race with fear. I felt my palms start to sweat, and my feet felt heavy as if I was rooted to the spot. It was as if I could feel the weight of the moment bearing down on me as if this was the last day of my life.

In a moment of panic, I blurted out, "Shut up. Are you mad? Don't say anything to her."

Aadhya turned to face Shantanu and asked with a hint of curiosity in her voice, "Yes, Shantanu. What happened? Are you looking at me?" Her gaze then shifted towards me, and she recognized me, exclaiming, "Hey! You're the one who got scolded this morning."

Feeling embarrassed, I simply replied, "Hi," wondering how I had built such an unflattering image of myself.

Shantanu interrupted my thoughts, saying, "He has to ask you something. Will you take him with you?" As I stuttered, trying to come up with an answer, Aadhya teased me by asking, "What? Where do you want to go?" I stumbled over my words, barely managing to say "w-w-w-w...". Aadhya encouraged me to continue, saying, "W-w-w... Say it."

Realizing I couldn't go through with it, I nervously replied, "Nothing, nothing. He's just kidding."

Aadhya, seemingly amused, asked for my name, to which I responded, "My name is Atharv."

"Oh, nice name! New admission, right?" Aadhya asked with a friendly smile.

I replied, "Yes, yes," feeling relieved that the conversation had taken a positive turn.

"Okay, welcome to our school, Atharv," Aadhya said before bidding me goodbye and leaving.

And after talking to Aadhya, I found myself humming a tune, unable to get her out of my mind. The words flowed out naturally,

"A girl I met, a beautiful rare

Her smile, a light that warms the air In her eyes, a spark ignites a fire

A girl I met, my heart's desire."

As I continued to hum the melody, I felt a sense of excitement. Shantanu's stern voice interrupted my daydreaming, "Get up.

What kind of mischief are you getting into? Have you gone crazy?"

Feeling shy, I tried to compose myself and explain the situation to Shantanu, "Shantanu, I am experiencing a feeling of butterflies in my stomach and a sense of completeness." However, it seemed like he didn't understand what I was saying.

He replied, "This question is finally done. What were you saying?" Feeling awkward, I simply replied, "Nothing," and began to smile, relieved that the awkward moment had passed.

And then the class started, but I don't know what happened that day, but it was very special for me.

I had no idea what was happening, it was a new emotion in my life that I had never felt before. I had friends before, but this feeling was different. It felt like there was a sense of happiness inside me like they were cutting sugarcane in the background.

Shantanu said, "Listen, we will go home together, and I will show you my coaching."

I replied that it was fine and asked him about his mother.

Shantanu said that soon his grandparents would be joining them, and hopefully, they would figure it out.

Summer Vacation

"The summer heat had set in, and along with it, my studies had commenced. As Shantanu had warned me earlier, the subjects weren't a cakewalk, and fate had decided to test me further." "During my coaching session today, I was seated behind the girl who had made a joke about me earlier."

At first, I tried not to pay attention, but soon enough, I realized that it was the same person. I had seen her before in her school uniform, but now she was dressed in casual clothes, looking stunningly beautiful. It was almost like she was an apsara, a heavenly nymph, and my eyes followed her every move.

Shantanu, who had been observing my reactions, said, "You should have been paying more attention to your studies." I felt a little irritated at his comment. "What?" I asked him.

"I am saying, focus on the laws of motion, not emotions," Shantanu replied with a hint of amusement in his voice. "Is that the same person?" I pointed to the girl in front of me.

Shantanu nodded his head in confirmation, and I felt a sense of confusion. How had she ended up in the same coaching as me? Was she following me? These thoughts raced through my mind, and I couldn't focus on anything else.

"What happens to you when you see her?" Shantanu asked, his voice now tinged with concern. "I get the feeling that this girl is not right for you."

I felt a sudden pang of annoyance at his words. "Will you ever say anything positive?" I retorted, feeling irritated. "As an idiot, I'm just looking at her."

The class eventually ended, and as I was leaving, the girl suddenly called out to Shantanu. "Hey, Shantanu! Wait!" she said, her voice filled with excitement.

As I watched, Shantanu turned around to face Aadhya who had just asked him why he had not answered her phone call. Shantanu explained to her that the number she had called was not his personal number and hence he was unaware of the call. Instead of dwelling on the missed call, Aadhya swiftly changed the topic and extended an invitation to Shantanu for her upcoming birthday party.

However, Shantanu informed her that he was not aware of the party and had a doctor's appointment scheduled for the evening. He seemed apologetic for not being able to attend.

Aadhya then expressed her understanding of Shantanu's situation and concern for his mother's health, wishing for her speedy recovery.

"I was standing on the side and listening to their conversation. Honestly, I was expecting Aadhya to invite me as well, but she didn't. My mind started to wander, and I began to wonder how Aadhya knew about Shantanu's mother's health condition when he had only mentioned that he needed to attend an appointment.

Moreover, the fact that this person has her number too added to my curiosity.

As Aadhya departed, Shantanu looked at me with a perplexed expression and voiced his confusion, "Why did she invite me?" I responded with a tone of frustration, "Yeah, it does seem strange, doesn't it?"

I didn't want to elaborate on my own thoughts, but Shantanu could hear the annoyance in my tone.

"What's wrong with you?" he asked, concern etched on his face. I shook my head and avoided his gaze, muttering, "Nothing."

Shantanu didn't seem convinced by my response and probed further, "Come on, talk to me. Is something bothering you?

"However, I chose to ignore Shantanu's question and instead picked up my bicycle and headed towards my house."

Shantanu called out from behind Hey listen come with me, where are you going? I swear I really don't know But I was feeling a mix of emotions today - anger, jealousy, or maybe even confusion. I was angry that Shantanu hadn't told me anything or frustrated that the girl hadn't even noticed me."

Shantanu followed me, calling out my name. He stood outside my house and continued to call out to me.

After hearing Shantanu's voice, my mother came into my room and asked, 'What have you done now? Have you fought with Shantanu again?' She sighed and continued, 'When will you stop acting like a child? It's not a good sign.

Upon hearing my mother's words, I stormed out of the house and confronted Shantanu, "Why are you shouting? Can't you come to my room instead?"

Shantanu expressed his concern and said, "Why didn't you respond when I was calling out to you? Is there something bothering you? Why did you leave in such a rush and with anger? You are my closest friend, and it's important for me to know what's going on with you. Please tell me."

After listening to him, I pondered to myself, "What's his fault?" Instantly, I felt ashamed of my dismissive response to Shantanu. However, I realized that I needed to rectify my mistake. Therefore, I apologized to him and said, "I'm sorry. I was preoccupied with my thoughts and didn't intend to be dismissive. You're right, and I shouldn't have reacted that way."

However, it seemed like Shantanu understood my confusion, and he explained, "My aunt and her mother are friends, so she found out about my mother's health through her. And in 8th grade, we worked on a bell ring project together. Do you remember that time when I missed three cricket matches for the project? That's how she got my mother's number."

I turned to Shantanu and mustered up the courage to speak, "No need to say this, I feel sorry for my behavior." Shantanu's eyes softened as he looked at me and responded, "Still, if there's a doubt in the friendship, it's better to solve it rather than just thinking about it without any reason."

His words hit me hard. He was right. I had been so consumed by my thoughts and insecurities that I let it affect my friendship with Shantanu. I bowed my head and whispered, "I was ashamed of my actions today."

Shantanu smiled reassuringly and said, "No need to be ashamed. We all have bad days. See you tomorrow." With that, he left me to ponder over his words and the importance of communication in any relationship.

Now I was feeling really bad about my actions, and I had decided that the next day I would tell Shantanu about my feelings and how I felt about Aadhya.

The following day, I arrived at Shantanu's house two hours ahead of our coaching session, hoping to engage in a sincere conversation and address any lingering doubts. Upon reaching his house, I learned that the scheduled evening appointment had been canceled the previous day, prompting Shantanu and his mother to visit the doctor in the morning. Shantanu's grandmother advised me to wait for him in his room, so I settled in, hoping for an opportunity to speak with him.

However, as time ticked away, and with approximately one and a half hours of waiting, I made the difficult decision to leave. Hastily bidding farewell to his grandmother, who sat in the living room, I headed towards the coaching center. As I cycled my way there, my worst nightmare unfolded—my bicycle suffered a flat tire. Attempting to fix it, I soon realized that the process was taking longer than I could afford. Aware of the significance of the coaching session, I made the difficult choice to leave my bicycle at a nearby shop and rushed towards the coaching center.

Panting and drenched in sweat, I finally reached the coaching center, aware that I had arrived late. I entered the coaching center, and it came as no surprise that it was already bustling with students. The hall reverberated with the lively chatter of voices and the rhythmic turning of pages. With a sense of urgency, I swiftly scanned the room in search of an available seat, only to find that every chair was occupied. Left with no alternative, I begrudgingly settled for a spot at the back of the hall, where the visibility of the board and the audibility of the teacher's instructions were compromised.

I made a valiant effort to concentrate, straining my senses to absorb the knowledge being imparted. However, the distant location and the cacophony of noise made it arduous to grasp the intricacies of the subject matter. Despite my best attempts, comprehension eluded me, slipping through the gaps in my understanding like sand through clenched fists.

Eventually, the coaching class drew to a close, and a tinge of disappointment washed over me. The opportunity to expand my knowledge and improve my understanding had been marred by my late arrival and the unfavorable seating arrangement. Resigned to the circumstances, I embarked on the journey back home, opting to traverse the familiar path on foot.

It was scorching hot, exacerbating my frustration and anger due to the lack of understanding during the coaching class. As I stood there, feeling the heat bearing down on me, a sudden relief came in the form of someone pulling up on a scooter next to me and asking if they could drop me somewhere. The stranger's eyes, hidden behind dark sunglasses, and the rider, wrapped from head to toe in layers of clothing, resembled an ancient Egyptian mummy, meticulously shielding themselves from the scorching sun.

I asked, "Who are you?" The scorching heat seemed to intensify the curiosity in my voice.

Removing their sunglasses, the mysterious rider looked at me reassuringly and said, "Don't be afraid. I am Aadhya, a fellow student from your school."

I chuckled lightly and replied, "Oh, yeah, I know you." Then, I continued with my response, "No thanks, I appreciate the offer, and assured her that I'm not afraid. It just seemed a bit unusual, that's all." Pausing for a moment, I continued, "I prefer to make my way on my own. However, I do have to make a quick stop to pick up my bicycle along the way."

Aadhya's eyes sparkled with understanding, and she let out a joyful laugh. "I completely understand," she said, her laughter lingering in the air. "Independence is important. But if you were to fall due to sunstroke, you might miss out on my offer. So, come, I'll drop you off there."

I joined Aadhya in laughter and agreed to her offer.

I boarded Aadhya's scooter, and as we embarked on our journey, she began to inquire about my educational background. Her curiosity seemed insatiable as she delved into a series of questions. She asked about the school I attended in 10th grade and my academic marks during that time, whether I was preparing for the JEE (Joint Entrance Examination), and the extent of the syllabus covered in my section. Her enthusiasm for details was palpable, but it felt overwhelming.

Sensing my slightly overwhelmed state, I gently interrupted her barrage of questions. "Take a moment to breathe," I suggested, hoping to ease the intensity of the conversation.

Aadhya paused, her exuberance temporarily subdued and offered an apologetic smile. "I'm sorry," she said, laughter tinging her words. "I tend to get a little carried away with my talkative behavior."

I smiled back, appreciating her self-awareness and lightheartedness. "No worries," I reassured her. "It's just a lot of information to process all at once. Let's take it one step at a time, shall we?"

With a nod of agreement, Aadhya shifted the conversation to lighter topics, allowing me to share snippets of my journey through academics and aspirations. As we navigated the bustling streets, her genuine interest and infectious laughter created a comfortable atmosphere, turning what could have been a daunting journey into an unexpectedly enjoyable experience.

As we arrived near the shop where I had parked my bicycle, a wave of disappointment washed over me as I realized it was closed. Aadhya, ever perceptive, noticed my dismay and quickly offered reassurance. "Don't worry," she said, her voice filled with warmth.

"Come back in the evening. The shop will be open then."

Grateful for her understanding, I considered my options. After a moment's thought, I expressed my desire to continue the journey on my own. "Yes, I'll go on my own from here," I replied, expressing my appreciation for her earlier assistance.

"It's okay," Aadhya said, her smile radiating kindness. "See you tomorrow."

Her parting words filled me with a sense of anticipation and left an imprint on my heart. With a final exchange of pleasantries, I bid her farewell, conveying my genuine gratitude. "Yeah, sure. Bye..."

Walking away, my mind was consumed by thoughts of Aadhya. Her presence had transformed what started as an ordinary day into something extraordinary.

Just as I was deep in thought, I noticed Shantanu walking towards me. He greeted me warmly and inquired about my day at coaching. Intrigued by his genuine interest, I decided to open up a little more and asked about Shantanu's mother, wanting to know how she was doing. Shantanu, however, replied, "I'll tell you about that later. Right now, I want to hear your side of the story."

Appreciating his eagerness to listen, I shared the details of the coaching class, highlighting my struggle with understanding the concepts. Aadhya's name naturally slipped into the conversation, as she had been the one to offer me a ride earlier. Shantanu listened attentively, his eyes filled with curiosity and a touch of familiarity.

After hearing me out, Shantanu paused for a moment, gathering his thoughts. His voice carried a hint of wisdom as he began to speak. "Aadhya's nature is like that," he said, his words carrying a weight of experience. "I've known her since 6th grade, and she's not the type of girl you think she is."

His statement intrigued me, and I leaned in closer, eager to understand his perspective. Shantanu continued, his tone thoughtful, "She may come across as moody or mysterious, but beneath that exterior, she's a fascinating blend of complexities. She's fiercely independent, passionate about her interests, and has a unique way of looking at the world."

As I absorbed his words, a mix of curiosity and intrigue enveloped me. Aadhya's enigmatic nature seemed to captivate those who knew her well. Shantanu's insights hinted at a depth beyond the surface, inviting me to discover more about the layers that composed her personality.

In that moment, I realized that my encounter with Aadhya had only scratched the surface.

I felt a pang of disappointment in my heart but Shantanu's words of wisdom brought me back to reality. "If you still feel that way, then you should ask her because these feelings might cause you problems in the future and you won't even know it."

With those words, Shantanu left me to ponder his advice. Thanking Shantanu for his perspective, I bid him farewell and continued on my way. The thoughts of Aadhya lingered in my mind, igniting a sense of intrigue and excitement for the journey ahead.

As I walked home, I felt a sense of clarity and determination. I knew that talking to Aadhya was the right thing to do, and I couldn't wait for the opportunity to do so.

But on the other side, my mind was in a whirlwind of confusion and uncertainty too. The question that relentlessly echoed in my mind was: What should I say to her? Should I delve into the realm of romantic feelings and ask if she likes me or even loves me? The mere thought of broaching such a topic felt foreign and unsettling, accompanied by a wave of nervousness.

Contemplating the best approach, I realized that perhaps it was premature to jump directly into matters of the heart. Instead, I could focus on building a stronger friendship and connection with Aadhya, allowing our bond to naturally evolve. It was essential to cultivate a solid foundation of trust and understanding before delving into deeper emotions.

With this realization, a sense of relief washed over me. I didn't have to rush into defining our relationship or professing my feelings just yet. Instead, I could embrace the present moment and enjoy getting to know Aadhya on a deeper level, allowing our connection to grow naturally.

With all these thoughts running through my mind, I decided to take out my book and start doing my homework. It was a way to distract myself from the confusion and uncertainty that were consuming me.

As a teenager, I think it is common to experience a range of thoughts and feelings related to the opposite gender. Navigating these emotions can sometimes be challenging, and finding the right person for guidance and support can feel difficult.

During this phase of life, it's important to remember that it's normal to have questions and uncertainties about relationships and romantic feelings. Many teenagers go through similar experiences, and it can be helpful to know that you're not alone in your journey.

The next day, as I made my way to coaching, my mind was solely occupied with the thought of how to express my feelings to the girl I liked. There was little room for any other thoughts as I walked toward the coaching center.

During my journey, I engaged in a conversation with my friend Shantanu and inquired about his mother's health once again. He informed me that she was scheduled for an operation in Hyderabad in a couple of days, and they were all hoping for her recovery. I replied with confidence, "Of course, she will recover."

Upon reaching the coaching center, we settled down to discuss our homework, and to my surprise, Adhya chose to sit next to me. The significance of her decision to sit beside me felt immense at that moment, and it stirred up a mix of excitement and anticipation within me.

Feeling a surge of nervous energy, I greeted Adhya with a friendly "Hello." However, instead of acknowledging my presence, she turned her attention to Shantanu and asked him, "Why didn't you come to coaching yesterday?"

I couldn't help but feel a sense of confusion and disappointment. It seemed as though she didn't even remember me, and her focus was solely on Shantanu. It left me wondering why she was acting this way and why our previous interactions didn't seem to hold much significance to her.

Shantanu quickly responded, "I was at the doctor's with my mother."

Adhya replied, "Okay, I pray to God she will be fine soon." Her response showed her concern for Shantanu's mother, but it didn't extend to me or our previous interactions.

As the class began, the topic of discussion shifted to the states of matter. Our teacher proceeded to explain the various aspects of the matter, but throughout the lesson, he seemed to notice that I appeared somewhat down. With a touch of amusement in his voice, he jokingly asked, "Atharav, what's the matter? Did you lose something or someone that's got your heart all broken?"

I responded with a smile, trying to downplay any hint of personal turmoil, "No, sir. Nothing like that."

However, the teacher's jest didn't stop there. He playfully turned towards Aadhya, wearing a mischievous grin, and asked, "Aadhya, did you say something to him?"

Aadhya, seemingly caught off guard, swiftly replied, "No, sir. I don't even talk to him."

The teacher then proceeded with the class, leaving me to reflect on the exchange. It became apparent that the teacher and even Shantanu glanced at me with a smirk and laughed. The way Shantanu laughed made it clear that he was right for Aadhya.

After the class, the teacher made an announcement that there would be a one-week break from coaching, and the school would also be reopening soon. He encouraged us to make the most of our holiday and enjoy ourselves before we had to return to our studies. The class expressed their gratitude to the teacher for the information, and with a sense of anticipation, we all left the coaching center, excited about the upcoming break.

As we were leaving the coaching center, Adhya asked me about my bicycle and if I still needed a lift. In the midst of my emotional turmoil, the confusion and uncertainty overwhelmed me. Frustration took hold, and without thinking, I looked at her and replied, "No, I don't need any help."

In that moment, my words may have come out of frustration.

Upon reflecting, I found myself thinking, "This girl has a way of playing with my feelings. One moment, she is kind, offering me a lift, and the next moment, she acts as if she doesn't even know me. I couldn't make sense of her behavior, and it left me feeling confused and upset."

Aadhya expressed her confusion, her face displaying a perplexed expression. She queried, 'What is there to be angry about in this? In fact, you should be thanking me for yesterday's incident instead of getting angry with me.'

I responded, 'You're welcome for the assistance, and I agree with you. When we lend a helping hand, it's best not to continuously bring it up.'

Aadhya argued, asserting, 'I'll speak as much as I want; it's my choice.'

I replied, 'Exactly, it is your choice. You have the freedom to express yourself when you feel the need to, and likewise, you can choose to ignore when you prefer. However, it's important to consider that I am also human, and your words can affect me emotionally. We can either move on from this incident or, if you wish to discuss it further, let's have a proper conversation. I would prefer to avoid this back-and-forth conflict. Do you understand?'

Aadhya turned her gaze towards Shantanu and questioned, 'Why is your arrogant friend yelling at me? What's wrong with expressing myself? I will speak up when I feel like it.'

Shantanu responded, "I don't want to be involved in this. Why are you two behaving irrationally, fighting without any valid reason?"

Amidst the tense atmosphere, Aadhya's words echoed in the air, I'm also not interested in this pointless fight. If this is how it's going to be, then no, I don't want to talk to him anymore. He looks like a monkey to me. If he is so angry, then why doesn't he climb a tree and eat some mangoes there?"

(Shantanu chuckled)

After that, Aadhya started her scooter and said, "Hey monkey, go find a tree for yourself during these holidays," with a smirk, and then she left.

I didn't have anything to say.

Shantanu said, "Relax, man. You're taking this too seriously. She's always been like this. I think you should just keep it as a friendship."

I remained silent and without saying anything, I went home.

It was the first time someone had judged me based on my looks. No friend had ever said anything like that to me before. And it's sensitive when someone calls you by a certain name because it makes you feel different and you start questioning yourself and wondering if you should change.As I stood in front of the mirror, lost in my own thoughts, my mother noticed my peculiar behavior.

Concerned about my behavior, my mother approached me and asked what had happened and why I had been standing in front of the mirror, acting like a monkey since morning.

Feeling bothered by the subject, my mother brought it up once more. Frustration overcame me, and I shouted, "Where do you see me as a monkey? I don't have a tail and my face is not monkey-like, so how did I become one?

My mother, undeterred by my outburst, responded with a soft chuckle, "Your behavior, my dear." She went on to explain, "Why are you letting this anger consume you? Even if I were to call you a monkey, would you transform into one just because I said so? When someone mocks you based on your appearance, you should simply laugh it off and respond, 'Yes, you're right,' and the matter will be resolved. Dwelling on such comments will only bring unnecessary stress upon yourself."

As my mother spoke, her words seemed like scattered puzzle pieces that I struggled to fit together. Though I couldn't fully grasp the meaning behind her advice, her comforting voice acted as a soothing balm to my troubled soul.

Feeling a deep sense of relaxation, I chose to immerse myself in the art of gardening, dedicating my time and attention to nurturing my garden with utmost care and affection. As I carefully tended to the plants, witnessing their growth and transformation, a profound sense of love and tranquility enveloped my heart. Surrounded by the captivating beauty of nature, I discovered solace and experienced a revitalized sense of joy that day.

2

A Day to Remember

The reopening of school brought forth a tremendous amount of pressure upon the students. Each morning commenced with rigorous math class, while the days concluded with the completion of practical files. The incessant titration experiments fatigued our eyes, and the physics derivations left our minds utterly drained. Every individual's thoughts became fixated on the impending exams, and the atmosphere crackled with tangible pressure. The students found themselves grappling to keep pace with the mounting workload as the exams rapidly approached.

During this period, the announcement of the syllabus set off a flurry of activity, as students could be observed gathering in the school grounds or library, earnestly immersing themselves in their studies to prepare for the forthcoming exams. The desire to excel and perform admirably loomed large, and each individual was resolute in making the most of the time at their disposal before the exams. They devoted extra hours to their studies and remained steadfast in their pursuit of completing the syllabus within the allotted timeframe. The library and grounds buzzed with the fervor and determination of these students, all driven by a shared goal.

However, among the students, there exist distinct categories. Some prefer to study in their own groups, while others seek guidance from teachers to clarify their doubts. Additionally, there is a group that focuses more on non-academic activities, such as discussing bike stunts. Lastly, some students cope with the pressure of exams by engaging in lighthearted joking and having fun. Each group handles the stress of upcoming exams in its own unique way. I joined a gossip group where I met Shubham, Iti, Ayushi, Karan, and Anamika. As we were engrossed in our lively conversation, Anamika unexpectedly mentioned that she knows my grandfather too. In that moment, I realized the significance of my words and the need to be cautious. Personal connections can bring an added layer of sensitivity, prompting me to carefully choose my words to avoid any unintended consequences.

Nevertheless, amidst our conversation, laughter filled the air, binding us together. We found solace and temporary respite from the mounting exam pressure, cherishing the camaraderie and joy that enveloped our interactions.

Aadhya approached the group, her face filled with curiosity. She had heard the laughter and chatter and wanted to know what was happening. As she neared, her eyes fixed on Anamika, and she inquired about a post that had caught her attention on Facebook. Aadhya's curiosity piqued, she wondered if the post was captured in the picturesque town of Shimla. Anamika swiftly responded, clarifying that the post was actually from Auli, not Shimla.

Shubham, seizing the opportunity to tease Aadhya, playfully remarked on her continued use of Facebook despite the looming exams. Aadhya, unfazed by the comment, coolly replied, "Well, it helps me keep my mind fresh." Her response echoed her belief in the importance of maintaining a balanced approach, finding moments of relaxation amidst the rigors of exam preparation.

The group, undeterred by the upcoming exams, continued their lively conversation and shared stories. Laughter echoed through their interactions as they delved into the realm of gossip, momentarily escaping the weight of academic pressures. Aadhya, fully engaged, listened attentively to their anecdotes, cherishing the sense of belonging that enveloped their discussions. In each other's company, they found solace and camaraderie, creating cherished memories amidst the challenging times.

With a smile, Aadhya turned her gaze towards me and asked, "How is your exam preparation going?" I replied, "It's going well. Then I added, 'You all continue with your conversation. I'm going to find Shantanu. I wonder where that lazy guy is hiding.'" Aadhya, displaying her enthusiasm to accompany me, said, "I'll come with you too."

It wasn't unusual; by now, I had grown accustomed to her unpredictable moods. So, I casually responded, "Yeah, sure, let's go." As we strolled across the school grounds, Aadhya turned to me and asked, "Are you still angry with me?" I paused for a moment, searching my memory, and replied, "Honestly, I don't remember being angry with you at all."

Aadhya looked at me with a concerned expression, as she continued to ask, "Is everything okay between us? If you're not angry with me, then why did you change your coaching timings?"

I replied, "I don't know, I just felt like it was the right thing to do."

Aadhya nodded understandingly, "I see. But I hope we can still be friends, I don't like the idea of anyone being hurt.

I reassured her that there were no underlying issues or conflicts between us. However, I admitted that my feelings for her went beyond just friendship. Seeing her at coaching sessions would often distract my mind and hinder my ability to concentrate on my studies. I explained that switching to morning coaching had its advantages, such as smaller class sizes and easier access to clearing doubts.

Aadhya teased with a playful smile, "You can't concentrate on studying when you look at me? Does that mean there's something more going on?" I responded, trying to hide my slight embarrassment, "No, it's not like that. I just feel that our connection goes beyond friendship, and it becomes challenging for me to stay focused when you're around."

Just as our conversation unfolded, Shantanu made an unexpected appearance, interrupting our moment. He jovially remarked, "Hey, you two! Are you going to study or keep hanging out like a pair of lovebirds?" We both shared a laugh and replied, "Actually, we were looking for you..."

Shantanu playfully interrupted, "The entire school is watching you two, and here you are claiming to be searching for me. Wow!" He chuckled and continued, "Come on, guys, exchange numbers and talk on the phone. Why are you wandering around like crazy people on the ground?"

Aadhya responded with a surprised "Oh!" to Shantanu's comment, her cheeks blushing slightly with a hint of shyness. Without uttering another word, she turned away and silently walked off.

As Shantanu's gaze met mine, I could sense his playful intentions. Anticipating his next comment, I swiftly interjected, "Come on, Shantanu, let's redirect our attention to solving math questions. It's time to focus and put an end to the teasing."

Caught off guard by my interruption, Shantanu's grin widened, acknowledging the validity of my point. "Yeah, you're right," he chuckled. "We should get back to studying." A burst of laughter escaped his lips, a testament to his ability to find humor in even the most lighthearted of situations.

As I pondered the decision of sharing my feelings with Aadhya, doubts and concerns filled my mind. I found myself questioning whether it was the right choice and worrying about how she would perceive me. The fear of potential consequences, such as a change in our communication, weighed heavily on me. However, I reminded myself to let go of these thoughts and maintain hope that everything would work out for the best.

Realizing the trap of overthinking, I decided to shift my focus to the upcoming exams.

During exams, I've noticed that our minds tend to wander to insignificant things. But when it comes to teenage love, I see it as both a curse and a blessing. The flood of emotions and thoughts that come with it can be overwhelming and uncontrollable.

And It would not be incorrect to say that the beginning of a healthy relationship starts with the ability to control those feelings, and that it is better to go with the flow rather than wasting time dwelling on them.

After some time, the exams ended and the results came in. Of course, Shantanu had topped in both sections. I remember a dialogue from the movie "3 Idiots" that goes something like this: "When a friend fails, it feels bad, but if a friend comes first, it feels even worse. Perhaps this is what they call 'sweet jealousy'

As the dust of the exams settled, the students began to excitedly share their scores with each other. Thankfully I didn't have many friends and wouldn't have to go through the embarrassment of sharing my marks.

But Aadhya, who seemed excited, was headed in my direction and I was trying to avoid her. As I was trying to sneak away, she called out, "Hey Atharv, where are you going? Listen to me. And all I could wish for was that she would ask me about anything other than my marks.

But she surprised me by saying, "We're going to have a party in the evening, and I thought it would be great if you and Shantanu could join us." I replied, "Yes, sure! I'll let Shantanu know, and we'll be there. Thank you for the invitation."

After that, it seemed like she didn't have anything else to say and there was an awkward moment where we stood there, smiling at each other without saying anything.

I said, "Okay," and with a hint of embarrassment in my voice, I asked, "Is there something else you want to say?"

No, nothing else to say," she replied, blushing. "Okay, bye," and with that, she walked away.

And I whispered to myself, "Atharv, don't overthink it and just go with the flow. Aadhya is a valuable friend, and I cherish our friendship. I don't want to jeopardize it by letting my thoughts and emotions cloud our bond." I took a deep breath, letting go of any unnecessary worries, and embraced the present moment, ready to enjoy the upcoming party and treasure the moments shared with my friends.

As I was lost in my thoughts, my friend Shantanu appeared in front of me and said, "Hey man, congratulations on your results.

You didn't even congratulate me." This made me realize that I had completely forgotten to congratulate him on his achievement and I immediately apologized and congratulated him.

But with a teasing grin on his face, what's going on between you and Aadhya? You two looked pretty cozy over there. What's the deal?" I tried to play it off with a casual grin, "Oh, nothing man. Just catching up, you know. Nothing to worry about."

Shantanu said, "Well, if your studies aren't getting affected, I don't see anything wrong with you and Aadhya being friends. But, be careful, because society tends to judge young people easily. Instead of judging, if they could guide us, maybe we (teenagers) would understand things better."

I agreed with Shantanu's viewpoint, acknowledging that he was mostly correct. However, I also added that if society promotes vulgarity and immorality under the guise of love, it becomes necessary to discern and critique such behavior. It is a delicate balance that we, as teenagers, need to comprehend and navigate.

Shantanu's eyes widened as he expressed his admiration for my perspective.

Then I said to him, "Listen, Aadhya invited both of us to a party."

He burst into laughter and replied, "Oh, I see. Yeah, it's at Iti's house."

And then, in surprise, I exclaimed, "Oh, bro! I completely forgot to ask where the party is!" Then Shantanu, while placing his hand on my shoulder, said, "You go crazy when you see her, don't you? That's all. Nothing more." And without dwelling on the topic any further, I changed the subject. I asked him, "How is Aunty doing?"

Shantanu replied, "She's not doing well. We're all worried about her health. My father is currently in Hyderabad with her. He says she's getting better, but we don't really understand the details. It's a bit concerning for the whole family."

I tried to reassure him, saying, "Everything will be fine. Just have faith in God."

At 5 PM, our group of friends consisting of Adhya, Shubham, Shantanu, Ayushi, Karan, Anamika, and myself visited Iti's residence. Iti hails from a Jain family. Upon entering the house, we were greeted by a statue of Lord Mahavir. Iti's mother, radiating warmth and hospitality, extended her heartfelt greetings and ushered us into the cozy confines of their home. With utmost grace, she presented us with glasses of cool, refreshing water, inviting us to quench our thirst and settle ourselves comfortably.

While Iti's mother had already acquainted herself with the other members of our close-knit group, my presence was an unfamiliar addition to her discerning eyes. Curiosity brimming within her, she kindly inquired if I had recently become a part of our convivial circle, expressing uncertainty regarding our prior encounters amidst our mutual companions.

Maintaining an air of politeness, I earnestly conveyed my name as Atharv, and she correctly predicted that I am a recent addition to the group.

In the midst of our conversation, Iti arrives and apologizes for being late. We all exchange amused glances and jokingly say, "Fashionably late, huh? No worries, we forgive you!"

Iti's mother pleasantly instructs us to proceed with our activities while she attends to some errands at the market. With genuine warmth in her voice and a radiant smile, she assures us that she will return shortly. We exchange nods of appreciation, recognizing the trust she places in us to carry on in her absence. As she bids us farewell and gracefully exits the house, we feel a sense of responsibility and profound gratitude for the opportunity to continue our plans and savor the enjoyable moments together.

Party Time

Girls often find joy in dancing at social gatherings such as functionsor parties, and they often excel in their dancing abilities. Their graceful moves and synchronized steps captivate the attention of the crowd, creating an atmosphere of liveliness and excitement.On the other hand, the boys in our group seemed content with observing one another's expressions and sharing lighthearted reactions among themselves.

As we enjoyed the festivities, engrossed in the delightful flavors of salty chips and samosas, holding a refreshing beverage in one hand and snacks in the other, we felt a sense of contentment.Suddenly, Iti proposed an unexpected idea, saying, "Why don't we all participate in a couples dance?"

"I was considering the positive atmosphere created by the meal and wondered why we should interrupt it with a dance, particularly a couple dance. I had entertained the idea of participating in a couple dance in my dreams, but when the opportunity presented itself, I declined and stated, 'No, this is not appropriate. It's not a suitable thing to do.'

In every party or group, there is always one person who ruins theatmosphere. And I felt that person was me at that party.

Karan managed the situation and said, 'Come on, guys, no problem. Whoever wants to dance can dance, and whoever doesn't want to can just relax.'"

Shantanu agreed with Karan and said, "Yes, that's right. Those who want to dance can dance, and those who don't want to can participate in other activities

For the couple dance, Iti and Karan were on one side, while Ayushi and Shubham were on the other. The rest of us cheered themon.

We witnessed an excellent dance performance however, it was challenging to determine which couple had danced the best.

After that, there were 2-3 activities including a game of Dumb Charades.

The party came to an abrupt end when Ayushi's father called her, signaling that it was time for her to head home. Throughout the event, I didn't get the opportunity to have a conversation with Aadhya, who had invited me to the party. Just as we were preparing to say our goodbyes, Ayushi urgently mentioned that she needed toleave and asked if someone could give Aadhya a ride home. Without hesitation, Shantanu chimed in and said, "Of course, Atharv can doit."

Upon Shantanu's suggestion, Karan volunteered and said, "No problem, I'll be heading in that direction anyway. I can drop heroff at her home." He looked at me and asked, "Atharv, is there any issue?"

In response, I replied, "You should ask Aadhya directly. At least find out if she wants to go with you.

Aadhya responded, "Why, Atharv, is there a problem for you if you drop me off?"

I quickly replied, "No, I don't have any issue with that. Last time, you kindly gave me a ride on your scooter. Today, it's my turn to return the favor. You can ride on my bike, and that way, we'll be even."

Aadhya glanced at Karan and replied, "All right, I'll go with Atharv. The rest of you can head home now. And Atharv, please make sure to drive carefully."

With Aadhya's decision made, it was clear that she preferred to accompany me for the ride. I acknowledged her request to drive safely, assuring her that I would be cautious on the road. With farewells exchanged and everyone else departing, Aadhya and I prepared to leave together, ready for a safe journey back to her home.

Aadhya and I continued in silence as we traveled down the road.After a while, Aadhya broke the silence by asking, "Is it true that youdon't enjoy dancing?"

I responded, "No, that's not entirely true. While I don't have a particular fondness for dancing, the truth is I was feeling a bit shy about it at the party."

Upon hearing this, Aadhya burst into laughter and exclaimed, "What shame? It was just dancing! They weren't asking us to get married or anything!\

I chuckled and replied, "Well, you're right. I suppose I was being a bit too self-conscious. On a side note, I also noticed that you are afantastic dancer, so you could have enjoyed it too."

Aadhya changed the topic and asked, "You were trying to tell mesomething on the ground that day, but you didn't say it. Why?"

I replied, "Aadhya, I apologize for not being able to express myself clearly that day. The truth is, I was struggling with finding the right words and the right moment to tell you what was onmy mind. I didn't want to rush into it or potentially create any misunderstandings. But please know that it's something important,and when the timing feels right, I promise I will share it with you."

Aadhya, teasingly, responded, "What time? You're so shy. You should have been born a girl."

And in this lighthearted manner, we arrived near Aadhya's home, both of us still laughing. Aadhya then requested, "Drop me off here so that the people in the neighborhood don't misunderstand. And if you have some time, feel free to message me. Do you have mynumber?"

I replied, "No, I don't have it."

Aadhya nodded and said, "Alright, then give me your number, and I'll message you when I have some free time."

As I walked away from Aadhya's house, a sense of happiness enveloped me, stemming from the brief but meaningful journeywe had shared. My mind was abuzz with a myriad of thoughts, questions, and revelations. The world around me appeared incredibly beautiful, and even the mundane sounds of people arguing, dogs barking, and traffic bustling seemed to harmonize into a symphony of life.

Arriving back at my home, I found myself humming tunes, a reflection of the joyous state of my heart. Each melody seemed to carry the echoes of our laughter and conversation. At this moment, I felt a deep sense of contentment, grateful for the connection I hadwith Aadhya and the newfound beauty I found in the world around me.

Mom asked, "What's the matter? The songs you're singing, your walk, and even your manner of speaking, everything seems different. Is everything alright?"

I simply replied, "Oh, I just came back from a party, Mom. That's the reason for my cheerful mood." With a smile on my face, I walkedinto my room, leaving my mother reassured but curious about the events of the evening.

A message popped up on my phone, and it was from Aadhya. Themessage read, "Have you reached home?"

In response, I swiftly typed, "Yes, I just arrived. Are you okay?"

As I hit send, a voice of self-reflection chimed in, questioning the contradiction in my words. But before I could ponder it further,Aadhya replied with a message adorned with a smiling emoji, saying, "Hey, we just met, and I'm absolutely fine."

Her response eased any lingering doubts and brought a smile tomy face, reassuring me that our encounter had left a positive impacton both of us.

As our conversation carried on, time seemed to slip away unnoticed, and before we realized it, the evening had progressed from 7 PM to 10 PM. Just then, my mom called out, breaking my engrossment, "Atharv, are you planning to stay cooped up in your room all day or come out and have dinner?"

I replied, "No, Mom, I'm not hungry. I already ate."

Assuring my mom that I had already satisfied my hunger, Iconveyed my gratitude for her concern.

Then Aadhya posed the same question through a text, "Did you eat?"

I responded, "No, I haven't eaten yet, but I'm not feeling hungry at the moment." Curiosity prompted me to inquire about her own meal. She promptly replied, stating that was feeling full. She mentioned that she was going to sleep, bidding me goodbye and wishing me to take care. She added, "See you tomorrow."

I replied, "Sure, take care and have a good rest. Bye." With that, our conversation came to a close for the night.

The next morning, during the assembly, our eyes met and we exchanged smiles. The smile had a different character, one that conveyed a feeling of serenity and satisfaction, as opposed to a grinthat was intended to tease or ridicule

During the recess, we started meeting and when we went home, we continued to chat. This is how it kept going

It seemed that our relationship was more than just friendship, but I still lacked the courage to confess my feelings to her.

As our interactions continued and our connection grew, it didn'tgo unnoticed by those around us. People began to observe ourfrequent meetings and exchanged smiles, and the students in our class started to speculate that there might be something more goingon between us.

Whispers and curious glances became a common occurrence whenever we were together. Our classmates, fueled by their own imaginations and perceptions, began to form theories and speculateabout the nature of our relationship.

And if someone finds a topic to gossip about, whether it's in society or school, they repeat it like a daily prayer.

People in this situation often begin to express their thoughts and opinions on why a particular boy or girl may not be suitablefor each other, despite their own personal shortcomings. They mistakenly believe that they have the power to judge and understand society.

Somewhere deep down, you know that they are talking about you, but you still try to ignore them and not pay attention to their gossip.

But what happens when someone comes to your table and asks you directly about it?

You can respond politely by saying: "I appreciate your interest, but I prefer to keep that information private."

If you do decide to share your feelings, you can express yourself in a clear and honest manner, such as saying: "I have feelings of love for someone." However, it's important to consider the potentialconsequences of sharing such information and to make sure you are comfortable with those consequences before doing so.

"I still haven't been able to express my feelings to the person I wanted to, but today I will gather the courage and speak up. This is what I thought before sending a text to Aadhya.".

My message to Aadhya was to inquire about her knowledge on the subject of love and if she would be willing to share her understanding of the appropriate age for experiencing love, as well as how one can determine if a potential partner is suitable or not.

After waiting for a response for two hours, I sent another message asking if she would be willing to share the information or not.

It was unusual because Aadhya usually responds within 5-10 minutes, but today I had been waiting for her reply for more than two hours.

I sent another message asking if I had asked her the wrong question, which is why she was not responding.

That night, I waited for her reply, but there was no response."

The next day in assembly, Aadhya ignored me, which was strange. I wondered if I had asked something wrong, and that's whyshe was not looking at me anymore. I started to feel like I shouldn'thave asked her that question.

Then negative thoughts started to arise like maybe her mother had read the message.

But only Aadhya could have provided the answer to all of these questions, as she was not present on the playground during the recess.

For a week, things were like that, she wasn't replying to messagesnor talking to me in school, and now it's irritating and frustrating tobe ignored by someone. This frustration has now turned into anger.A week later, I saw her in the library. I picked up a physics book that was kept there and sat next to her. I approached her and said,"Excuse me, Aadhya. May I ask what's going on? It seems like you'vebeen avoiding me for the past week. Is there anything I did wrong?

Could you please explain the situation to me?"

She sat there, unmoving, appearing as if she didn't hear me.

With a slightly louder voice, I asked, "Why are you remaining silent? Could you please share what's going on?"

The librarian gently reminded us, "Excuse me, are you here to read or to have a conversation? Please keep the books in their proper place and leave the library."

Aadhya suddenly burst into laughter and turned to me, saying, "What's the matter? Has it only been a week and you're already frustrated? Let's leave the library." And come with me.

I was taken aback by Aadhya's response. Confusion and surprisewashed over me as I tried to make sense of her words. Had she beenintentionally ignoring me as some sort of prank or test? Or was there a misunderstanding between us?

Curiosity got the better of me, and I decided to follow her, hopingto gain some clarity on the situation. As we left the library, I approached Aadhya, my mind still filled with questions.

Before I could utter a word, she spoke up, acknowledging my frustration and explaining that she had actually been answering myquestion. I felt a mixture of relief and curiosity as I eagerly awaited her explanation.

With my confusion still evident, I gazed at Aadhya and askedher to clarify her previous statement in simpler terms. I wanted to ensure that I fully understood her explanation and the meaning behind her actions.

Aadhya took a deep breath and looked at me earnestly. She beganto explain that her delayed response and apparent silence were not signs of ignoring or disregarding my message. Instead, she had beentaking the time to carefully compose a thoughtful and meaningful response.

She apologized if her actions had caused any confusion or frustration, assuring me that her intention was not to play games or joke around. She genuinely wanted to engage in a meaningful conversation and share her thoughts on the subject I had asked about.

She replied, "Atharv, you asked me about my understanding of love. If I'm being honest, I don't have much knowledge on the subject. However, what I do believe is that love encompasses patience, trust, and compassion. Love is like a butterfly that becomes even more gorgeous when given the freedom to spread its wings.

Curious about the concept of the age of love, I turned to Aadhya and asked for her perspective. She responded thoughtfully, saying, "The age of love is a deeply personal experience, unique to each individual who has felt its profound impact.

Perhaps you can inquire about the beginnings of love with your parents, asking them when they first fell in love with you. Did they have a specific age in mind, like 'I will love you when you are 5 yearsold,' or did their love transcend any specific timeframe?"

Aadhya's statement sparked a laugh from me, lightening the mood.

She asked, "Tell me, did they say that to you?"

I replied, "Of course not. Love is not bound by specific ages or conditions. It grows and evolves naturally."

Curious to explore further, I added, "And what about finding the right partner? How does one know when they have found them?"

Aadhya shared her perspective, stating that the definition of a "right partner" varies from person to person. She emphasized that individuals have diverse preferences when it comes to choosing a partner. Some may prioritize physical attractiveness, while others may value intelligence, care, financial stability, or other qualities. Itis subjective and unique to each individual's desires and needs.

When I inquired about Aadhya's perspective on the matter, she admitted that she hadn't given much thought to the specific qualities or traits she desires in a partner. However, she shared her view on love as a seesaw game. According to her analogy, both partners play vital roles and must work together. Just like in a seesaw, maintaining balance requires effort from both sides. Both partners need to push and pull, putting in equal efforts to sustain the relationship and keep the "game" of love going.

Aadhya further elaborated Suppose if one partner dominates and the other simply follows, it is likely that the relationship will not be sustainable over time. This type of dynamic could ultimately result in the end of the relationship. To maintain a healthy and balanced relationship, both partners must take turns pushing their self-respect to the forefront and pulling down their ego and dominance. This way, both partners can work together to keep the relationship strong and lasting.

Curious about Aadhya's understanding of relationships, I asked her how she came to possess such insights.

Aadhya responded, sharing that her parents had a love marriage,which might have contributed to her understanding of love and relationships. She playfully suggested that perhaps this knowledge could be passed down genetically, as she herself wasn't consciously aware of acquiring such wisdom.And then both Aadhya and I burst into laughter.

The librarian madam was looking at us for a long time. She camewith a stern look and told us to Go back to our class.

We both apologize and run away .

Shantanu saw us coming from the library and said "Hey Atharv,come here I want to talk to you."

Aadhya stated, "You may proceed with the conversation, I will beheading to my class now."

I inquired, "Shantanu, what do you wish to discuss?" Shantanu replied, "There have been some rumors circulating in the class regarding you and Aadhya. I just wanted to bring it to your attention." I responded, "I do not concern myself with such trivial matters. It doesn't matter to me what others might say." However, Shantanu added, "It's not just a matter of you not caring, it's about how it might impact your image in front of the teachers and what people might say about Aadhya as well."

I remarked, "We are merely friends, what is the issue with the class in this regard?" Shantanu, with a hint of irritation, stated, "It would be best if you keep this friendship out of the school premises.Furthermore, Anamika is also your friend. How much interaction do you have with her in the school environment? You have her phone number, how frequently do you communicate with her?"

I was at a loss for words, and Shantanu pressed further. "Atharv,look at me and tell the truth. Have you told Aadhya how you feel about her yet?"

I finally replied, "No, I haven't. I don't want to lose this friendship. And if it's meant to be, she'll let me know."

Shantanu smiled warmly and expressed his thoughts, "The decision is entirely up to you, my friend. I simply believed that it would be beneficial if you spoke to her directly. By doing so, any misunderstandings could be cleared up, and you would gain clarity. Honestly, I believe she's content with your presence as well. I've observed a noticeable change in her behavior since she met you. She has become noticeably more composed in class, engaging in fewer arguments and speaking less than before."

Based on these observations, I suggest that you initiate a conversation with her starting today and continue from there.

I replied, "Alright bro, I'll ask her "

As I reached home, I called Aadhya. Once she answered the phone, I inquired if she would be willing to meet with me tomorrow, as it is Sunday and Atlas Park is located near her residence. I wouldlike to have a conversation with her regarding a matter.

Aadhya asked what the matter was and said she could not come to the park. She suggested we discuss it over the phone instead.

I replied that it was the same matter I was unable to discuss withher that day on the ground.

She agreed cheerfully and informed me that she would come, but she would bring her mother along. She then chuckled and askedif it would be all right for her to accompany her mother.

I was speechless, thinking, "What should I say to her now?"

Aadhya said, "Don't worry, just relax. I'll come to the park; it's nearby anyway. If you say anything wrong, I'll beat you up. I have many brothers near that park."

I started laughing and said, "Yes, I will come prepared then. See you at 8 AM there." She agreed with the timing.

(Call hangup)

"The night passed by as I lay awake, my mind filled with anticipation and thoughts of what I would say to her the next day. In my imagination, I conjured up elaborate scenarios, akin to scenes from romantic movies, but the reality was that I lacked the financial means for grand gestures or the ideal physical appearance.Determined to set aside those grandiose thoughts, I eventually succumbed to sleep.

The following morning, the sun's gentle rays peeked through mywindow, rousing me from my slumber at 7 AM. I was about to headto the shower when my mother called out to me, her voice tinged with urgency. 'Listen,' she said, 'I need to go see the doctor. Can youcome with me and make an appointment by calling the doctor as soon as possible?'

I nodded, still groggy from sleep, and replied, 'Okay, fine. We'll go in the evening.'

My mother's response caught me off guard. 'No, in the evening, Ihave to go to the market with your aunt,' she explained. 'You shoulddo it now quickly, and we'll return on time.'

As I pondered her words, a glimmer of hope emerged within me. If I made the appointment for 10 AM, I could seize the opportunity to meet Aadhya before heading to the doctor's clinic. The thought filled me with joy, and I eagerly headed to the bathroom to take a refreshing shower.

After taking my shower, I immediately made the call to the doctor's office. A gentleman named Anil, who is a member of the doctor's staff, answered the phone and courteously informed me that the doctor would be leaving town today. Understanding the urgency of my situation, Anil kindly suggested that I come in as early as possible.

"I knew that if I told my mother that the doctor was going out oftown, I would have to go with her right away. If I didn't tell her andshe found out later, I would be kicked out of the house. I was very confused, but then I made the decision that it was better for me to go with my mother now."

I said to my mother, "Let's go, they have called us to come as early as possible.

I sent a text message to Aadhya letting her know that I might be running a bit late, but I realized that my SMS pack had run out andI had no balance left on my phone.

Mom shouted at me, "Come on, start the bike quickly. You are always stuck on the phone. Give me the phone,and she took my phone.

As I arrived at the clinic, I saw a large number of patients waitingto see the doctor. I couldn't help but wonder why so many people seemed to be sick on the same day.

I told my mother, "Let's come next time. You are looking fine to me. Anyway."

Then she said, 'Be quiet and stand here. I am going to ask them how long it takes for our number to be called and in between if you leave, I will tell your father and rest you know.

(It's already 8.30 now)

Our turn came around 9.15 and then we took medicine andreturned home from the clinic around 10 o'clock.

As soon as I dropped my mother off at home, I went straight to the Atlas Park and realized I had forgotten my mobile phone

As I made my way to the park, I felt a sense of unease. I was already 2.30 hours late and I feared that Aadhya may have already left. But I pressed on, determined to find her. I wandered aimlessly through the park, scanning the crowds for any sign of her.

Just when I was about to give up hope, I heard a voice call out my name. I turned to see Aadhya, standing there with a smile on herface. Her hair was disheveled, covered in the dust of the park, and her face looked weary. The sun had left its mark, casting a warm brown glow over her eyes and leaving her lips dry and parched. Buteven in this state, she was beautiful. She held a diary in one hand and in the other, a pen.

"Now you're here," she said, her smile never faltering.

I stumbled over my words, trying to apologize for my lateness.I explained about my mother and the errand, but she stopped me mid-sentence. Her eyes were like daggers, piercing into mine. "Whatdo you want to say?" she asked. "Why else would you come here, on this scorching afternoon, if you didn't have something important totell me?"

"And so, I took a moment to gather my thoughts, feeling a surge of courage as I prepared to speak from the depths of my heart. It was a message that had burdened me for far too long, and I knew I couldn't keep it locked within any longer.

With a deep breath, I closed my eyes, hoping to find solace in the darkness, and mustered the strength to utter the words that had been waiting to escape. "Listen, please," I whispered, my voice laced with vulnerability. "Will you turn back? I feel overwhelmed byshyness, but it's crucial for me to express this."

Trembling with a mix of anticipation and apprehension, I awaited a response. And as the seconds ticked by, I gradually openedmy eyes, meeting their gaze with newfound determination and sincerity. It was a pivotal moment, a leap of faith into the unknown, as I continued, ready to share the weight of my thoughts and emotions."

"Aadhya, from the very moment our eyes met, a magnetic force seemed to draw me towards you, much like the irresistible pull ofa falling apple to the ground. As each day passed, my love for you blossomed and radiated with increasing intensity, akin to the sun's gentle ascent, illuminating the morning sky.

You have become my missing puzzle piece, completing the intricate design of my life. Your laughter resonates within me likea melodious symphony, its rhythm intertwining with the very essence of my soul. The sparkle in your eyes and the tender touch ofyour hand leave me breathless, igniting an insatiable yearning for more.

Words fail to convey the profound impact you have had on me. You have become the reason behind my constant smile, the wellspring of my happiness, and the guiding light that brightens my path. I am eternally grateful for every precious moment we have shared, and I promise to forever cherish and love you with all my heart.

Now, with hope brimming in my heart, I must summon the courage to ask a question that has been burning within me. A question that holds the potential to deepen our connection and forge a beautiful bond. Aadhya, my love, will you do me the honor of being my girlfriend? Together, let us embark on a journey of love, trust, and shared dreams, creating a tapestry of happiness and bliss."

Aadhya stood there, her emotions evident as tears gently streamed down her face. Her gaze met mine, and in a soft, trembling voice, she whispered, "Note the date and time." I understood the significance of that request, recognizing the importance of capturing this transformative moment forever.

With a mix of anticipation and hope, I observed her nod, a silent affirmation that stirred my heart with indescribable joy. As she walked away, her response lingered in the air like a sweet melody. A single word, "Yes," is filled with a universe of love and promise.

In that precious instant, I realized the depth of our connection and the profound impact my words had on her. It was a confirmation that our feelings were not only reciprocated but shared with equal intensity. Overwhelmed with a sense of elation and pride, I held onto that memory, etching it deep within my heart. The time and date, Nov 20 at 11:13, forever etched in the chronicles of our love, became a symbol of the beginning of our journey together. It marked the moment when our paths converged, intertwining our lives in a tapestry of affection, trust, and shared dreams.

3

A Shoulder to Lean On

This morning was truly extraordinary, unlike any other. As I stepped out onto my terrace, I was greeted by the melodious symphony of birdsong. Their sweet tunes seemed to carry a senseof freshness as if they were heralding the arrival of a new day filled with possibilities.

I looked up at the sky and noticed something magical. The clouds seemed to be forming a shape that resembled a smile. It was as if nature itself was expressing joy and contentment, spreading a sense of happiness all around. The sun, radiating its warm and gentle rays, caressed my face like a soothing massage. Its comforting touch awakened my senses and filled me with a sense of warmth and tranquility.

Amidst this serene ambiance, I could faintly hear the distant sounds of devotional music and the call to prayer. These ethereal melodies seemed to float through the air, embracing everything around me. They were like a fragrant breeze, akin to the delicate aroma one experiences when encountering a blooming rose. At that moment, I felt a deep connection to the divine, as if the universe itself was whispering sacred secrets to me.Just as I was lost in this enchanting experience, my phone pop up with a message from Aadhya appeared, "Good morning! Are you still lost in your dreams or have you woken up?"

I replied, "Since the day you said yes, sleep has eluded me. Morning or night, only thoughts of you, my mind besieges."

Aadhya retorted, "Wow, that's a clever way to change the topic. Where do you come up with such cheesy lines?"

I replied, "Perhaps you have cast a spell on me, my dear," to which she replied with a smile emoji, "If you keep talking like this, I'll get diabetes at a young age from all the sweetness."

The conversation continued as she asked me about the possibility of scheduling her coaching sessions in the morning. I pondered her question for a moment, considering the implications it might have on our daily routines.

"Well, it's not a problem for me," I replied honestly, "but I recall you being part of the evening batch for your coaching. May I ask why you want to switch to the morning?"

She paused for a moment, seemingly thoughtful, and then replied, "If I schedule my coaching in the morning, it would free up our evenings to spend quality time together and have uninterrupted conversations. I don't want either of us to compromise on our studies if the timings clash."

Her words caught me off guard, revealing a level of seriousness and consideration for our relationship that I hadn't anticipated. It made me pause and reflect on the depth of her commitment. While it surprised me, I appreciated her thoughtfulness and genuine concern for our well-being.

After a brief moment of processing, I responded, "That sounds reasonable. If rescheduling your coaching to the morning allows us to have more dedicated time together in the evenings without any distractions, then I fully support your decision. Our studies are important, and finding a balance that works for both of us is crucial."

I was elated, not only because we were going to attend coaching classes together, but also because it was an idea that had originated from her.

And then it feels like a song started playing in the background
.... Love, love, in the air,

For Aadhya and Atharv, a special pair. Love, love, all around,

A bond so strong, never to be found.

And as I began dancing to the song with joy and happiness, my mother, who I didn't realize was watching, burst into laughter, wondering if I had gone crazy because I was dancing without any music.

Unbeknownst to me, my mother's eyes met mine, and in that moment, I couldn't help but smile. With happiness in my heart, I gracefully walked towards my school, cherishing the memory of our cheerful exchange.

In school, I discovered that I was not the sole observer of her activities, as she was also discreetly keeping an eye on me. Throughout the day, we engaged in a playful exchange, and during the assembly, she would mischievously point out my distractions, like my unkempt hair. These lighthearted interactions only served to strengthen our bond and brought us closer together.

As we continued to spend time together, I learned more and more about Aadhya's likes and dislikes, her hopes and dreams. I found that we had many things in common, but also some differences that made our conversations all the more interesting. For instance, I was always amazed by Aadhya's passion for music. She would often talk about her favorite songs and artists, and I loved listening to her as she described the emotions that each one evoked in her. In turn, I shared my love of novels with her, and we spent many evenings reading together and discussing our favorite characters and plots.

I have vivid memories of her favorite song, "Love Story" by Taylor Swift. It became a regular part of our routine, as she would play it for me at least three times a day. It was a joy to witness the way her face would illuminate with happiness as she passionately sang along to the lyrics. The way she connected with the music and shared her love for it with me created beautiful moments that I will always cherish.

Even though I didn't understand every word, I still love that song because of her.

I think it's normal when you love and care for your partner. Over time, you may find that some of their interests become your own and that you start to appreciate the same things that they do.

Every night before we went to bed, Aadhya and I would take turns telling each other stories. Sometimes, I would weave my own tales, creating characters and plot twists that kept her on the edge of her seat. Other times, I would read passages from my favorite books. But it wasn't just me telling the stories. Aadhya had a knack for spinning her own tales, too. She had a wild imagination, and her stories were full of adventure and magic. I loved listening to her as she described the worlds that she had created, and I could feel my heart racing as she described the danger and excitement that her characters faced.

One night, as I finished one of my stories, I noticed the disappointment in Aadhya's voice. "I don't like it when the hero dies," she said, pouting. "It's too sad and depressing." I smiled and reassured her that it was just a story and that the hero's sacrifice had helped to save others.

But I couldn't help but think about her comment later on. I wanted to make sure that the stories I shared with her left her feeling happy and inspired, rather than sad and disappointed. So, the next time I wrote a story, I made sure that the hero survived and overcome their challenges. As I read it to Aadhya, I could see the smile spreading across her face, and I knew that I had done the right thing.

Over time, I learned to adapt my storytelling to Aadhya's preferences, adding more uplifting and hopeful elements to my tales. And as we continued to share our stories with each other, I realized that it was this willingness to listen and learn from each other that made our relationship so strong and enduring.

That particular day stands out vividly in my memory. It was an ordinary day, without any particular significance or celebration in sight. Little did I know that it would be filled with a delightful surprise orchestrated by Aadhya.

During the recess period, I was casually strolling towards the canteen in the company of my friend, Shantanu. It was then that I encountered a girl named Shreya, who introduced herself as a friend of Aadhya's.

Shreya's voice was laced with frustration and anger, as if she had also been looking for me and was fed up with the hunt. At first, I felt very angry at the way she spoke to me, but I decided that it would be better to go see Aadhya instead of saying anything to her. I quickly excused myself and hurried back to my classroom.

Upon arriving at my classroom, I caught sight of Aadhya waiting for me outside the door, holding the tiffin box in her hand.

Her face had a smile and her eyes showed a sense of shyness as she said, "I brought idli sambhar for you, and here you are wandering around without even knowing."

I couldn't contain my happiness; it felt like I had sprouted wings. Tears filled my eyes with joy, and my ears turned red with that feeling.

Firstly, I said thank you to her, but my gratitude was accompanied by a stutter of shyness.

Aadhya smiled and said, "Ohh Atharv, why do you act like a girl sometimes? Let's sit down and eat quickly, I'm really hungry!"

And her words made me realize that she also hadn't eaten anything until then. And I asked her but why hasn't she eaten anything yet?

Aadhya told me that she had prepared the idli sambar early in the morning, so that we both could have it together during recess time.

And as soon as we sat down to eat, the bell rang indicating that the recess was over.

As I burst into laughter, unable to contain my amusement, the sound reverberated through the classroom. "Oh man, the bell had to ring now!" I exclaimed, half-amused and half-frustrated at the timing.

Aadhya turned her gaze towards me, her expression filled with a mix of understanding and a hint of disappointment. Sensing my realization, she spoke gently, "Take this lunch box with you home." With those words, she left for her own section, leaving me with a tinge of regret.

In that moment, it dawned on me how my laughter might have been perceived. I felt a pang of guilt for not fully appreciating the love and effort she had put into preparing the lunch box for me. Aadhya's gesture had been a genuine expression of care, and my laughter could have unintentionally undermined the significance of her act of kindness.

I have decided that after finishing school, I will talk to her.

As I stood outside the school gates, my eyes locked onto Aadhya as she approached me. My heart soared with happiness upon seeing her. With a curious expression, she glanced at me and inquired, "Hey, what are you waiting for? Is someone supposed to meet you here?"

"It's you!" I exclaimed, a wave of relief and happiness flooding over me.

Aadhya's face softened, a warm smile spreading across her lips. "Oh, I see. You were waiting for me?"

I nodded, feeling a sense of tranquility as I gazed into her kind eyes.

Aadhya's eyes widened in surprise. "Oops, are you really crazy?

What happened? Tell me."

I chuckled, shaking my head. "Nothing's wrong, I was just eagerly waiting for you."

Returning my smile, Aadhya responded, "Alright then, let's go for a walk." I expressed my gratitude for the delicious idli sambhar she had prepared earlier, and suggested that we try a new restaurant for a meal this Sunday. "How about exploring some new places together?" I suggested.

However, Aadhya's expression changed when she reminded me that we had our board exams in just three months. She explained that our current time schedule was made for a reason, and that we should focus on our studies until the exams are over.

Even though I couldn't shake off a tinge of disappointment, I respected Aadhya's logical reasoning. I made an effort to persuade her, emphasizing that a single day out wouldn't significantly impact our studies. However, Aadhya firmly held my hand and reiterated the importance of prioritizing our academic pursuits. Deep down, I comprehended her perspective and acknowledged the need to focus on our exams before indulging in leisure activities. With a sense of understanding, I agreed to postpone any outing plans until after the exams, aligning myself with her commitment to our studies.

From my perspective, those who claim that "we fall in love" may not be entirely truthful. In my opinion, it's more precise to say that "we grow in love." As I gazed at Aadhya, I recognized that my love for her had evolved over time. It wasn't merely based on her outward appearance; it was rooted in her intelligence, compassion, and determination. She was a person who resonated with my aspirations and dreams, and our shared passions further strengthened our bond.

As we walked around the school, I noticed how the sun shone on her hair, making it glow like gold. The birds chirped a melody that matched the rhythm of our footsteps. And as we talked, I felt my heart fill with warmth and contentment.

In that very moment, a deep conviction settled within me, and I realized that I wanted to spend the remainder of my life with Aadhya. I yearned to bring her happiness, shield her from adversity, and provide unwavering support. As we strolled back to school, our hands intertwined, a profound certainty filled my heart. I knew that we would confront any obstacles that crossed our path with resilience and unity, standing side by side, ready to face whatever challenges awaited us.

Afterward, when I reached home, I warmed up the idli sambhar that Aadhya had prepared for me and began relishing it. The soft and fluffy idlis paired with the aromatic and flavorful sambhar created a delightful combination, and I enjoyed each mouthful. Just as I was nearing the end of my meal, Shantanu arrived, and without any hesitation, he grabbed a plate and joined me in savoring the same delicious dish.

He took a bite and exclaimed, "Wow, this idli sambhar is really delicious, Aunty! You've outdone yourself!"

My mother, who had been in the other room, walked in and looked puzzled. "What are you talking about, Shantanu?" she asked. "I didn't make any idli sambhar today."

Shantanu's expression turned quizzical as he looked at my mother. "You didn't make it?" he repeated. "Then where did it come from?"

I could feel my cheeks growing warm with embarrassment. I didn't want to admit that I had taken it from Aadhya. But before I could think of a plausible explanation, my mother asked again, "Yes, where did you get it from?"

I responded, attempting to steer the conversation away from my previous blunder, "Oh, I actually picked it up on my way home from school. There's a new shop that recently opened, and I wanted to give it a try."

Shantanu started laughing and asked, "Which shop is it? I want to try it too!"

I stammered out an answer, trying to think of the right words. "Um, it's just on the way back from school. I'll show you where it is tomorrow, Shantanu. Is that okay?"

Shantanu chuckled and replied, "Absolutely, I'm always game for exploring new flavors!" With a sense of relief, we concluded our meal, and I silently expressed gratitude that my small fib had passed unnoticed.

As soon as my mother retreated to her room, Shantanu gently tapped my shoulder, capturing my attention. He looked at me with a serious expression and said, "Atharv, things have reached this point, and you haven't even been honest with me. Aadhya gave you this, didn't she?"

I refused, shaking my head and said, "No, I bought it from the shop.

Shantanu sighed and said, Aadhya has also taught you how to lie, hasn't she? You're not the same anymore, my brother.

Realizing that I couldn't hide the truth from him, I apologized and said, "I'm sorry. You guessed it right. Aadhya gave it to me."

Shantanu playfully teased me, a smirk on his face as he said, "Looks like I'll have to start calling Aadhya sister in law now, huh?

I blushed at Shantanu's teasing and responded, "Oh, come on Bro, It's not like that's something we need to worry about right now. I still have to concentrate on my studies and find a good job before I even think about talking to her family or anything like that.

Shantanu then said, "So, have you already thought about the names for your future children?" and started laughing uncontrollably.

I said to him, "Enough, how much longer will you tease me? And tell me, did you come here just to eat my idli sambar or did you have some other reason?

He said, "I was just going to get some sample papers. I thought I would take you along with me, that's why I came here."

"I apologized, saying, 'Sorry, bro. I can't come right now because I'm already running late from school, and I have an important test tomorrow that I need to study for. However, if you let me know three hours from now, I'll be able to join you.' Shantanu informed me that he had a coaching session in an hour, so I suggested that he go to the market now, and I would meet him there later. I instructed him to find a shop along the way and buy a magnetic locket so that I could give it to Aadhya."Shantanu's face lit up with a smile, and he embraced me warmly in a hug, conveying his understanding and support.

As Shantanu hugged me tightly, he expressed his happiness for me. His words carried genuine warmth and sincerity. "I am happy for you," he said, his voice filled with joy. And then he added, "I will pray to God that Aadhya and you always stay together." He assured me that it was okay, and he would bring the locket for me on his way back. He insisted that I didn't need to come along and should focus on preparing for tomorrow's test.

Curiosity sparked within me, and I couldn't help but inquire, "Shantanu, what happened? Is everything fine?"

With a reassuring smile, he replied, "Nothing to worry about, my friend. I'm just feeling good about being responsible for my friend."

And then he left, leaving me to sit down with my book to study.

After studying for two hours, my phone rang, signaling a call from Aadhya. Excitedly, I answered, and without hesitation, I exclaimed, "The idli-sambhar you made was absolutely delicious! I shared it with Shantanu, and we both enjoyed it."

To my surprise, Shantanu had even given me a compliment. Today, he expressed that I had undergone a remarkable transformation in my character and had become more positive in life. It was the first time he had praised me in such a manner, and it brought me immense happiness and contentment. His recognition of my personal growth was truly uplifting and reinforced my determination to continue striving for self-improvement.

Shantanu's playful remark brought a smile to my face. "Should I start calling Aadhya my sister-in-law now?" he jokingly asked. Taking the lighthearted banter further, he even suggested that we begin contemplating baby names.

Aadhya chuckled at his comment and playfully responded, "He says all these things, but he always acts so innocent in class." In defense of my friend, I replied, "Indeed, he may come across as innocent, but he's my closest companion. He speaks to me with sincerity and honesty, and I value our friendship greatly."

Aadhya then added, "Yes, I have known him since we worked on a group project together in 8th grade. We recently reconnected in 11th grade after all these years."

Curious, I asked Aadhya if Shantanu ever talked about me, to which she replied that he hadn't spoken much about anything from the start. She added that Shantanu was always reserved and quiet, much like me, his friend.

I nodded and shared with Aadhya how Shantanu and I became friends and eventually became like brothers. Aadhya responded, "Okay, that's enough. You already told me that. Now it feels like Shantanu is your girlfriend."

Hearing this, I laughed and replied, "No, he means more to me than a girlfriend."

Aadhya said, "Do you know that you should never compare anyone with anyone else? It can make someone feel bad about themselves." She added that some people may take such comparisons in a negative way.

It seems like the hint was enough for me to understand that she felt bad about what I said. So, I tried to change the topic and said, "Do you know how beautiful your eyes are?"

Aadhya said, "No, no, why me? Shantanu has beautiful eyes, you should admire them instead."

And I chuckled and said, "Oh, sorry. I'll be more careful from now on. But you shouldn't be jealous of this."

Aadhya said, "No, why should I be jealous? He came into your life first, he is your best friend. I understand that, so don't worry. I was just pretending to be upset, it's nothing."

I was taken aback and asked, "Pretending? Why?"

Aadhya replied, "Oh, Atharv, you too? You do it because it feels good to be angry and fight." She explained that sometimes people engage in playful banter and pretend to be upset to add excitement or humor to a situation. It was her way of teasing and having a lighthearted moment. Understanding her intentions, I chuckled and realized that it was all in good fun.

The conversation continued as I was talking with Aadhya on the phone when suddenly, my mother entered my room looking worried. "Listen," she said anxiously, "Shantanu has had an accident." My heart dropped as I asked, "What? When and who told you?" Without even hanging up the call, I hastily put the phone in my pocket and ran out of my room, heading straight for Shantanu's house.

"Mom, said, 'Don't go now, wait for your dad to come and go with him.' But I didn't listen to her and ran towards his house."

As soon as I reached Shantanu's house, his father and uncle were frantically making arrangements for blood that was being called from somewhere. I approached his father and asked, "Uncle, what happened? Where is Shantanu?" He reassured me that Shantanu had only sustained a minor injury and that there was no need to worry. They were just making arrangements for blood donation. Meanwhile, my father also arrived at the location and took charge of the situation.

He told me to go back home since he was there and then he went to talk to Shantanu's father.

"But I said no, I will also come along," I replied. Shantanu's father then said, "Atharv, you go. Your dad is here, and we will take care of the arrangements. Don't worry."

In that moment of panic, I knew that not listening to Shantanu's father's advice would only make things worse, so I tried to understand their perspective and went back home.

Once I got there, I asked my mother who had told her about the accident. She told me that the milkman who delivered milk to Shantanu's house had informed her.

Seeing me sad and worried, my mother tried to console me, saying, "Don't worry, everything will be alright. God will protect him." However, my heart was still troubled, and I couldn't shake off the feeling that something might go wrong. My hands and feet were cold, and I longed for reassurance, but all I felt was anxiety.

My phone was ringing with 'Hello, hello' and then I remembered that Aadhya was still on the call. I asked her if she had heard anything, and she said, 'Listen, calm down first, don't panic. Listen to me, everything will be fine.'"

I said, " we were just discussing him, and now this news came up.

She replied yes. Just pray for him instead of getting anxious. I replied with a simple "Yes" before hanging up the call.

That entire night, I couldn't sleep a wink. All I wanted was to know that Shantanu was alright. I anxiously waited for my father to return home and give me an update on Shantanu's condition. Fear and uncertainty consumed me, and every passing moment felt like an eternity. The thought of something going wrong plagued my mind, and I longed for reassurance.

My mother noticed that I was awake and gently advised me, "Try to get some sleep. I'll wake you up when your father comes back home."

I said, "Can you try calling him and see if he picks up? He's not answering my calls."

My mother replied, "Yes, I talked to them. They said they will come home soon, and everything is fine there. Now go to sleep peacefully."

And when I heard that, I felt relieved and went to bed to sleep peacefully, thanking God for the good news

After sleeping for two to three hours, I woke up and went outside. I asked my mother if Dad had come back home, and she replied, "Yes, he came back. But you have to go to school now. You have a test today, right? Come back, and we will talk then. Now go quickly."

After a few hours of sleep, I made my way to school. As I approached the assembly area, I saw our principal, Mrs. Basu, standing there. Initially, I thought she was going to deliver another one of her lengthy speeches, but then she made a grave announcement - the school was closed for the day due to the passing of one of our brightest students, Shantanu, who was no longer with us.

The news hit me hard, and I couldn't believe what I was hearing. Just last night, my mother had reassured me that everything was fine, so why was the principal saying that Shantanu was no longer in this world? Aadhya looked towards me and gestured to calm down, but I was too overwhelmed and immediately left to go back home.

When I arrived home, I bombarded my mother with questions, demanding to know why she had told me Shantanu was fine when clearly he wasn't. However, my mother remained silent, leaving me to grapple with the reality of what had happened.

My frustration boiled over, and I began shouting at my mother, accusing her of lying to me. "You said everything was fine, but now the principal is saying something else entirely! Why would you lie to me like that?"

My mother remained silent, her face contorted with sadness and guilt.

As I walked towards Shantanu's house, I felt a sense of regret wash over me. I had said some hurtful things to my mother before leaving, and now I would never be able to take them back. But as I approached Shantanu's home, my regret turned to horror. His family had already taken him to the cremation ground. I felt like the world had just crumbled beneath my feet. I was in disbelief, my mind struggling to accept the truth. I had lost my best friend, and I hadn't even been there to say goodbye. As I made my way back home, my tears flowed uncontrollably. I locked myself in my room, overwhelmed by the weight of my grief.

I pounded my fists against the wall and screamed, feeling the sting of guilt and regret clawing at my heart. I cried myself to sleep, wishing for nothing more than the chance to turn back time and make things right.

Someone was banging on my door very loudly, and when I woke up and opened the door, I saw that it was my father standing there. I looked at him and started crying. What were his parents like?

Should I go meet them now? Had they already come home?

My father told me that his parents had left for Hyderabad from there, and it was not right for me to go there now. He asked me to calm down."

But then I told my father that Shantanu asked me to come along. He said those words to me. After hearing this, my father hugged me and said gently, 'Be quiet now, I can't bear to see you cry.

My father had seen him sitting with me in the second class, and the pain my father felt upon knowing him was as intense as the pain I experienced.

My dad suggested that I should eat something, but I refused, saying that I would tell him when I feel hungry. Then, my mom advised me to eat something to feel better, but I replied by stating that I would inform them when I feel hungry. My dad then gestured toward my mom, indicating that she should leave me alone.

Meanwhile, memories of Shantanu flooded my mind like a vivid flashback. I remembered his last hug, his behavior, and his talks. It all played out like a movie in my head, and I was lost in my thoughts. I was overwhelmed with emotions, and it seemed like all my complaints and grievances were directed toward God. At that moment, I questioned the divine plan and the higher power that governed our lives. I raised my eyes toward his side seeking answers to the endless stream of questions that plagued my mind.

"Why did you let this happen?" I asked, my voice trembling with emotion. "You are omnipotent and all-knowing. Everything in this world runs on your commands. So why did you allow this tragedy to take place?"

As I poured out my heart, I wondered if God even existed or if he was just a figment of my imagination. It felt like he was not aware of our pain and suffering, as if he was indifferent to our struggles. Perhaps, he did not comprehend the immense agony and torment we were going through. After all, Shantanu had barely lived a fraction of his life, and yet he was taken away from us so abruptly. After crying all morning, my lips had become parched from thirst and hunger. The corners of my mouth were cracked, and the skin felt tight against my teeth. As I lay there, exhausted from the effort of sobbing, I began to feel a dull ache in my eyes. The pain was like a weight that pulled at my eyelids, making them heavy and difficult to keep open. Eventually, the fatigue caught up to me, and I drifted off to sleep, my mind still consumed by the sorrow and pain of the morning's tears.

The next morning, my mother woke me up and told me that someone had come to see me. I replied that I didn't want to meet anyone, but then my mother revealed the person's name Aadhya and my heart skipped a beat. She said that she is waiting for me downstairs and handed me a glass of water, urging me to drink it and let go of my anger. "How long will you stay mad?" she asked, sounding exasperated. "I didn't lie to you. I just wanted to tell you when the time was right." With a sigh, I took a deep breath and a sip of water, still feeling angry As I made my way downstairs.

Aadhya was waiting for me on the couch when I arrived downstairs. I asked her why she had come and how she had found my address.

With a gentle gaze, Aadhya met my eyes and revealed that she had come specifically to see me. She went on to explain that she had reached out to one of her friends who happened to know where I lived, and they had kindly provided her with the necessary information.

Soon after, my mother also joined us with a cup of tea for Aadhya. The three of us sat quietly in the living room

My mother thanked Aadhya for coming and asked if she also knew Shantanu. Aadhya replied, "Yes, he was my classmate, Aunty.

Mom said, Aadhya will you explain to Atharv that no one comes back from being hungry and thirsty all the time.' Then, with tears in her eyes, she left the room

Aadhya said, 'Atharv, look at me once. Do you really think that the pain of Shantanu leaving is only yours? Are you doing this because you think it will bring Shantanu back?

I was still quiet and calm. Aadhya got up and came to me, and she lifted my head upwards.

Tears started flowing from my eyes, and then Aadhya wiped them away with her hand and said, 'Maybe all of this is hurting you right now, but to tell you the truth, Shantanu is probably hurting more from seeing you like this. Not only are you causing yourself pain, but you are also troubling Shantanu's soul by being unhappy.' By not eating your food, you are making your mother cry as well. Do you realize that? Remember what Shantanu said?

He never wanted you to be like this. He said that you have changed and that you cannot give up like this. I told her that he had asked me to go with him, and then I refused. This is what is bothering me.

Aadhya's eyes were filled with compassion as she listened to me. She held me close and whispered, "I understand your pain, but you need to be practical. Going with him won't change what has happened. You need to take care of yourself and not let your emotions consume you. Your parents love you, and they will be hurt to see you like this."

Her words resonated with me, and I knew she was right. I needed to take responsibility for myself and not let my grief control me. Shantanu wouldn't want me to give up on myself, and I promised to honor his memory by being strong and resilient, just like he always believed I could be.

I first apologized to my mother for the pain and hurtful words I had caused her. I knew I had been acting selfishly and not considering how my actions were affecting those around me. I took responsibility for my mistakes and said sorry for the pain I had caused.

My mother looked at me with tears in her eyes and hugged me tightly. "I forgive you, my child," she said. "I just want to see you happy and healthy again."

Her words filled me with warmth and comfort, and I knew that I had taken the first step toward healing. I realized that my loved ones were there for me, and I could count on them for support and guidance. It was time to let go of the pain and start anew.

"After apologizing to my mother, I decided to seek forgiveness from the divine for my foolishness. I prayed to God and expressed remorse for the hurtful words I had said and the pain I had caused. I then made a request to God to provide a peaceful resting place for Shantanu's soul. I asked Him to grant Shantanu a place in His heavenly abode and to comfort his loved ones who were still grieving.

As I prayed, I felt a sense of calm and tranquility wash over me. It was as if a weight had been lifted from my shoulders, and I knew that I had done the right thing.

I made a vow to myself to cherish the memories of Shantanu and to honor his legacy by living a life that would make him proud. With the love and support of my family and Aadhya, I knew that I could overcome any challenge and emerge stronger than ever before."

Such is the nature of our relationships that we often take our loved ones for granted, and it is only in their absence that we realize their true worth.

I remember the times when Shantanu and I would joke around, and I would tease him by saying that I would throw a party after his death. I never thought that those words would become a reality and that I would have to say goodbye to my dear friend.

But in his absence, I understood the importance of his presence in my life. Shantanu was not just a friend but a confidant, a support system, and a constant source of joy and laughter.

His loss left a void that could never be filled, and I often found myself reminiscing about the good times we had shared. I realized that life was too short and that we must cherish the moments we spend with our loved ones, for we never know when we might have to say goodbye.

Shantanu will always hold a special place in my heart, and I will honor his memory by living a life that is full of love, kindness, and compassion.

As time passes, wounds do tend to heal, but the pain of not having closure or clarity about a past event may still persist. Forgetting such events is not easy for a person, but they learn to manage and cope with their emotions, even if they don't express them on a daily basis. Despite everything appearing to have returned to normal, a deep-seated fear had taken hold in my life - the fear of losing someone.

After the incident, Aadhya became increasingly concerned about me. The schedules and timings that she had set were no longer being followed, and she would call or message me at any time. Our conversations were mostly related to the courses we were taking at that time. Aadhya was my girlfriend, but she had also filled the void left by my friend Shantanu quite well.

With her efforts, I began to forget about the pain of the incident. Aadhya's care and concern had a healing effect on me, and I found myself opening up to her in ways that I had never done before. She listened patiently to my problems and provided a sympathetic ear whenever I needed it. As we spent more time together, I found myself feeling more and more comfortable in her company.

Despite the trauma of the incident, I felt a sense of peace and contentment whenever I was with Aadhya. Her presence seemed to chase away my fears and anxieties, and I knew that I could always count on her for support and encouragement. I felt truly lucky to have her in my life.

To appreciate her efforts, I decided to go and pick her up from her home to the coaching center. Aadhya used to attend coaching with her friend "Iti" who also studied the same subjects as us. I thought it would be a nice gesture to go and receive her, and show her how much I valued her presence in my life.

Next day

As the sun began to rise over the quiet streets, I found myself standing outside her house at the godly hour of 5:00 AM, filled with excitement and anticipation to surprise her. But fate had other plans in store for me. My heart sank as I noticed Iti standing there, waiting for Aadhya.

Disappointment washed over me, and a sense of resignation started creeping in. Just as I was about to turn back and leave quietly, a mix of surprise and curiosity gripped me when she called out to me in a voice that seemed to reverberate throughout the entire colony.

"Heeey Atharv! Are you here to pick up Aadhya?" Her exclamation landed on me with unexpected force, leaving me momentarily stunned. It felt as if her words had delivered a sudden jolt, making my heart race with a mix of surprise and uncertainty. I found myself grappling to formulate a response, my mind racing to find the right words amidst the whirlwind of emotions swirling inside me.

Putting on my best smile, I approached her, trying to act casual. "Oh, hey Iti," I said, hoping to sound nonchalant. "What are you doing here?"

Iti's eyes sparkled with amusement as she looked at me. "I thought your house was near the coaching center," she said, her tone teasing. "But you live here too? Wow!"

I remained silent, unsure of what to say. Iti continued to chatter on, clearly enjoying herself. "I had heard that you live in Model Town," she said. "Do you think you've forgotten the way, or did you just come to pick up Aadhya?"

I nodded, trying to play along. Iti's laughter echoed in the early morning air. "Awww, dude, you are so romantic!" she exclaimed. "Okay, so wait here for her. She'll be out in a minute."

With that, she hopped onto her scooter and rode away, leaving me alone in the street with my thoughts. I was excited and nervous at the same time, wondering what Aadhya would think when she saw me. Would she be happy to see me? Or not?

As I stood there, lost in thought, I felt a pang of fear. What if someone saw us together? What if they told others in the society? But despite my anxiety, I couldn't deny the thrill of anticipation that coursed through my veins. I was about to see Aadhya again, and nothing else seemed to matter.

After a few minutes of anxious waiting, I saw Aadhya's familiar figure approach from the direction of her society gate. My heart began to race as she drew nearer, and I felt a rush of adrenaline course through my veins.

As soon as she spotted me, her face lit up with a radiant smile. "Atharv!" she exclaimed, her eyes shining with excitement. "Oh my god, you're here! You know what, after I woke up this morning, my heart was beating so fast, and I couldn't shake the feeling that you were nearby. And now, here you are!"

Her words were like music to my ears, and I felt a warmth spreading through my chest. "I had to see you," I said, unable to hide the smile on my face.

Aadhya's eyes sparkled with amusement. "You're such a romantic," she teased, taking my hand in hers. "But come on, let's go. We don't want to be late for coaching."

With that, we set off on my bike, and I felt an even greater surge of happiness as I rode alongside her, savoring every moment of her company. The wind rushed past us, carrying with it the scent of the morning air, and I felt grateful for this moment, this perfect, fleeting moment that I would always remember. Aadhya held onto me tightly, her arms wrapped around my waist, and I felt a sense of deep contentment wash over me.

As we reached the coaching center, Iti, and some of our mates were already standing in front of it. When they saw me alongside with Aadhya , some of them looked at me with jealousy, while others teased me with the sound of "woohoo."

I could feel their eyes following us as we walked past them, and I felt a little self-conscious. It was as if we were in a movie, and I was the lead actor walking alongside the most beautiful girl in the world.

It actually happens that even if the world sees you as Kadar Khan, but in your own story, you are the only Shahrukh Khan.

"When Aadhya asked Iti why she hadn't come to receive her, Iti replied, 'Your Romeo was there, and you know how much I hate playing the villain in someone else's movie,' she said, looking directly at me."

At first, I thought she was angry with me, but my confusion disappeared when she laughed,"

With all these lovely moments, it seems like the only thing trying to scare us is our upcoming exams. However, before the exams, an announcement was made about the farewell party. As soon as the word 'farewell' was uttered, the entire class erupted in excitement.

Why do people get so happy at the mere mention of a party? It's hard for introverted students to understand this phenomenon. Trying to explain the joy of social gatherings to them is like trying to teach a cat to swim - it's just not going to happen!

As the upcoming farewell party drew nearer, Aadhya's excitement grew, and she shared her plans with me. She eagerly described the saree she planned to wear, along with matching earrings and accessories. As one of the introverted students, I felt the opposite. The mere thought of being in a crowded room, making small talk, and pretending to have fun drained me of energy. Though I didn't dislike people, my social battery depleted quickly, and I needed alone time to recharge. I envied those who could easily blend in and enjoy social events, but I was not one of them.

When Aadhya asked me about my outfit for the party and expressed her excitement, I had to disappoint her by saying that I wasn't going to attend. I didn't get a chance to clarify my reasoning before she urged me to come with her. She was thrilled at the thought of us going together, and she didn't want to go without me. I told her that she should go and enjoy herself with her friends, as I didn't have anyone to go with. I asked her who I would even go there for.

For a moment, there was silence on the other end of the phone. Then, Aadhya spoke up again. 'Atharv, why do you think you don't have any friends? I am your friend too, and I want to wear that saree for you. Please come with me, otherwise, I won't go either.'

Her words caught me off guard, and they sounded so casual that I found myself agreeing with her. I said okay don't go and hung up the phone

I wasn't angry, nor did I completely disagree with her, but the way I expressed my reluctance to attend the party may have come across as rude due to my natural tendency towards introversion.

After our phone conversation ended, Aadhya sent me a text message. Her kind words warmed my heart. The message was, "Don't worry, Atharv. If you don't want to go to the party, I won't go either. But please, never say that you don't have a friend. I am your friend too, and I am with you anytime. Please don't feel low.

Her words made me realize how fortunate I was to have her. Her words and actions showed me that her love wasn't just about attending events or having fun together. It was about being there for each other, even when it meant making sacrifices or compromising on plans. But as an introverted person, the idea of attending a social event still made me nervous, but I didn't want to let Aadhya down. Besides, I realized that it was time for me to step out of my comfort zone and try something new.

Aadhya was thrilled when I told her that I would be joining her. She helped me pick out an outfit.Her positive energy was contagious, and before I knew it, I was actually looking forward to the party.

When we arrived, the venue was buzzing with activity, and I felt overwhelmed by the crowds. But Aadhya stayed by my side and introduced me to her best friends who are now studying commerce. As we mingled and chatted, I realized that it wasn't as bad as I thought it would be. I even found myself enjoying the conversations and laughing along with everyone else.

Aadhya looked absolutely stunning in her black saree, captivating the attention of everyone around her. As she moved through the crowd, I noticed the envious looks from boys. It seemed like they were all wondering why Aadhya had chosen me.

Suddenly, Karan appeared and asked Aadhya to dance with him. My heart sank as she turned towards me, and I felt a flood of emotions. I wanted to punch Karan for even daring to ask, but instead, I put on a fake smile and said, "Sure, let's dance. It's a farewell party, and maybe we'll not see each other again after exams, right?"

As Aadhya and Karan danced, Shreya came up to me and whispered, "Do you know that Karan likes Aadhya? And you still sent her to dance with him?"

A knot formed in my stomach why she said this to me like this? I had sent Aadhya to dance with someone who had feelings for her. I didn't know what to say to Shreya, so I just nodded silently and continued watching Aadhya and Karan.

Iti joined in and teased me, saying, "Hey Atharv bro, you look pretty cool in that suit. I bet Aadhya helped you choose it, didn't she?"

I blushed at her comment and tried to hide my embarrassment by shaking my head. While it was true that Aadhya had helped me pick out the suit, I wanted it to remain between us. It felt like a personal moment, and I didn't want anyone else to intrude. So, I just awkwardly smiled and tried to change the subject.

I said to Iti, "You look beautiful too." Then Iti said, "Don't take Shreya's words to heart, Atharv."

I replied confidently, "No, Iti, I'm not bothered by it. After all, I trust Aadhya." But I am surprised by her words.

Iti chuckled and remarked, "Dude, she acts like Komilika, the villain character in Kasauti Zindagi Ki. Her nature has always been like that. But hey, why are you here? Go and dance with Aadhya." With a playful nudge, she pushed me towards Aadhya and cheered loudly, "Atharv, Atharv!"

Afterward, Aadhya and I started to dance together as a couple. She whispered in my ear, You should have declined and broken his face. I smiled and said, 'It's okay. Besides, you are so beautiful that everyone would want to dance with you.'

She interrupted my thoughts and said, "Don't use those cheesy words, okay? You're the one who makes me feel beautiful." Her words took me aback, and I felt a rush of emotion. I smiled and pulled her closer, feeling grateful to have her in my life. Dancing with her felt like the most natural thing in the world, and I knew that I never wanted this party to end.

We were lost in each other's eyes, and we didn't even realize it when our principal arrived at the party. It was as if we were in our own little world, and nothing else mattered. But suddenly, we saw our principal walking towards us, and we quickly composed ourselves. It was a surprise to see her at the party, but we greeted her with a smile and continued to enjoy the party.

The principal smiled at us and said, "Oh, you both look so lovely together. Like Radha and Krishna." Hearing her words, I felt a surge of happiness within me. It was nice to see that our principal was not as strict as we had thought or maybe she didn't want to ruin our party.

After that, we took some photos with our teachers and got their blessings. It was a great feeling to have their support and encouragement. Finally, it was time to head back home. We said our goodbyes and promised to keep in touch, and then we parted ways, each heading back to our own homes with memories that would stay with us forever.

So I said, "Aadhya, let's go. I will drop you off." Then she interrupted, saying, "Hey, wait. I have something for you. Please close your eyes." Naturally, I responded, "What? No, tell me what prank you want to pull on me." Aadhya persisted, "Trust me."

Reluctantly, I allowed her to cover my eyes with her hands, uncertain of what she had in store. However, I decided to put my trust in her. I could feel her hands moving, searching for something. Then, she placed a small object in my palm. Opening my eyes, I discovered a beautifully crafted locket with the word "Love" delicately inscribed on it.

I was surprised and touched by her thoughtful gesture. I thanked her and asked, "What's this for?" Aadhya replied, "Just a little something to remember me by." I smiled and said, "I could never forget you stupid.

We hugged each other tightly, and in that moment, everything felt perfect. It was like time stood still, and nothing else mattered except for the warmth of her embrace. I could feel her heartbeat, and I knew that mine was racing just as fast. It was as if we were two puzzle pieces that had finally found each other, and there was a sense of completeness that washed over me.

As we pulled away from the embrace, Aadhya looked at me with a smile on her face and said, "I hope you like it."

I smiled back and said, "I love it. Thank you so much."

We walked towards my bike, and I helped her put on the helmet. As we rode towards her home, I felt grateful for this beautiful moment. I knew that it was just the beginning of something special, and I was excited to see where this journey would take us.

4

A Taste of Rituals

⸺◆♡◆⸺

Aadhya and I were playing in the clouds, relishing our time together. We laughed and danced, immersed in the ethereal beauty that surrounded us. Suddenly, she turned to me with determination in her eyes and said, "Listen, I will go and fetch some water from those black clouds. You prepare the house with these white clouds. "I nodded, intrigued by her suggestion. "Yes, I will prepare the house," I replied, watching her glide gracefully toward the darkenedclouds. As I started shaping the white clouds into the form of a cozy cottage, a sense of excitement and anticipation filled the air.

However, our idyllic moment was interrupted by an unexpected turn of events. The sky darkened, and heavy snowflakes began to fall from above. Confusion enveloped me as I pondered how it could snow amidst the clouds. It was then that I realized we were in heaven.

As I was trying to process this realization, I saw a man approaching me. He looked familiar, almost like my father. I cautiously inquired, "Hello, who are you?" The unfamiliar individual responded, "The results are out today."

I was taken aback and asked, "What results? Where is Aadhya?" I recollected that she had gone to fetch water from the black clouds. I worried about her well-being. "She had gone to get water, right?" I inquired of the stranger.

I then noticed that his appearance was unsettling. He bore a striking resemblance to a kidnapper. I exclaimed, "I thought you were a God, but you resemble a kidnapper. Where is my Aadhya?"

Unexpectedly, the stranger forcefully grabbed me and hurled me away. In the midst of falling, I cried out, "Oh God, save me!"

And then I opened my eyes, startled and disoriented. I saw that my father was standing at the foot of my bed, looking at me with a mixture of concern and amusement. It took me a moment to realize that I had fallen off the bed in the midst of a vivid dream.

"Hey Atharv, are you awake yet?" he asked, his voice filled with warmth and affection. "It's already noon, and the sun is directly overhead. Will you come out of your imagination and face the real world?"

I rubbed my eyes and tried to shake off the lingering haze of the dream. Then I remembered the reason for my father's urgency. "Oh, Dad, I almost forgot. Today is the day my exam results will be released. Do you think I passed?"

My father chuckled and ruffled my hair. "Of course, you passed, my boy. You've always been a diligent student. Now get up, brush your teeth, and come down for some breakfast. You need to be ready to face whatever the day brings."

I smiled at his confidence in me, but I couldn't dismiss the lingering unease brought on by the dream. "Dad, you won't believe the dream I had last night. You appeared as a kidnapper, wearing a wide, unsettling grin."

My father burst out laughing at my words. "A kidnapper? Me? I think you've been watching too many movies, son. But don't worry, your dear old dad won't kidnap you. You're stuck with me for life."

As my mother entered the room, she looked at us with a quizzical expression. "What's so funny?" she asked, her tone filled with curiosity.

My father chuckled and filled her in on the details of my strange dream. "Atharv here dreamt that I was a kidnapper, and he was trying to escape from me," he explained, a twinkle in his eye.

My mother rolled her eyes and shook her head. "That's ridiculous. Atharv, you've become so lazy after the exam. I don't know how you're going to survive in college when I'm not around to keep an eye on you," she chided me, her tone tinged with concern.

And we both start laughing by seeing her expression

My father and I exchanged a mischievous glance, knowing exactly what was coming next. We both burst out laughing, unable to contain our amusement at my mother's reaction.

My mother gave us a mock glare, but her lips twitched in amusement despite herself. "What's so funny?" she asked, a hint of exasperation in her voice.

"Nothing, Mom. We're just teasing you," I said, still chuckling.

My father nodded in agreement. "That's right. You worry too much. Atharv is all grown up now, and he can take care of himself."

As my mother returned to the kitchen, she remarked, "This son is just like his father."

I exited my room, took a refreshing shower, and enjoyed brunch before heading straight to the computer to check my results.

However, my excitement quickly turned to frustration as I discovered that the website was overloaded with traffic, and my anticipation was met with a spinning circle that refused to show me my marks.

As I waited anxiously for the website to display the results, I was a bundle of nerves. I knew I had done well in the exams, but the fear of the unknown was almost overwhelming, making it difficult to focus on anything else.

Finally, after what felt like an eternity, the website released the results. I quickly checked my marks, and to my immense relief and joy, I had passed! A scream of happiness escaped me as I celebrated my accomplishment.

As I shared the news of my exam results with my parents, their faces lit up with joy. They thanked God for my success, and I felt grateful for their love and support.

I had heard that on the day of exam results, relatives tend to call to inquire about your performance. However, I didn't receive a single call from any of my relatives. It made me wonder if my relatives were exceptionally considerate or if their own children's results were disappointing.

But I was still waiting for the call from the person I was expecting to hear from, and that call still hadn't come.

So, I decided to take matters into my own hands and make the call myself. Without wasting any more time, I dialed Aadhya's number and waited anxiously for her to pick up.

And then the phone was picked up and before she said hello and I launched into an explanation about my dream and how I had been waiting for her call. Suddenly, a voice from the other end of the line interrupted me. "Hello? Who is this?"

I was taken aback for a moment, wondering who could be calling you. Then, a mischievous idea popped into my head. I decided to have a little fun.

"Who am I?" I said, trying to sound flirty. "Baby, you forgot about me already? It's Atharv, silly!"

"Atharv, Aadhya is not at home. She has been summoned to the school for a photo session as she has achieved the top position," the voice on the other end of the phone informed me. It was at that moment I recognized it was Aadhya's mother speaking.

Feeling remorseful, I quickly responded, "Oh, aunty, I apologize. It was just a joke, and I'm sorry." Aadhya's mother chuckled and reassured me, saying, "It's okay, Atharv," before ending the call.

Feeling relieved that Aadhya's mother wasn't upset with me, I took a deep breath and smiled to myself. I was looking forward to congratulating Aadhya on her achievement and hearing more about her photo session.

Later, my mother came into the room and asked me about the girl who had come over on that day. "How did she do in her exams?" I replied, "Aadhya topped in school, Mom! She's really done well." My mother smiled and expressed, "That's wonderful news. Please pass on my congratulations to her when you have a chance to speak to her."

I replied, "Yes, sure."

Just as I finished speaking, my phone rang once again, and it was Aadhya calling. I swiftly answered the call and greeted her, saying, "Hello, Aadhya."

She responded, "Hey, did you talk to my mom?"

I replied, "Yes, I spoke to your mom earlier. I thought it was you, so I shared everything I wanted to tell you."

Aadhya laughed and replied, "It's okay, Atharv."

After congratulating Aadhya for her outstanding achievement as the school's topper, she appeared delighted and expressed her gratitude. However, she followed up by suggesting, "Why don't you come over to my house and congratulate me in person? You can also meet my parents. My dad is at home today."

I smiled and enthusiastically agreed, "Sure, I'll come over. See you soon."

We bid our farewells and ended the call. I felt excited about the prospect of meeting Aadhya's parents.

As I walked towards Aadhya's house, I couldn't help but wonder if this was all real or just a dream. But as I reached her doorstep, I realized that it was not a dream, and I was really there to meet her.

I contemplated that perhaps Aadhya's family was open-minded and accepting, which is why they welcomed me to their home. Considering her parents' love marriage, they might not adhere strictly to traditional beliefs. It was possible that they didn't place much importance on factors like caste, religion, or societal norms. I reassured myself, saying, "Chill, Atharv. You're here as a friend, nothing more."

I rang the doorbell, and Aadhya's mom opened the door, offering a warm smile and inviting me inside. It became evident that her parents were truly liberal and open-minded. They greeted me with genuine warmth, instantly making me feel comfortable and at home.

As we sat down and engaged in conversation, my worries dissipated. Aadhya's family was no different from any other loving family, showing no concerns about my presence. We discussed various topics, and I wholeheartedly congratulated Aadhya on her remarkable accomplishment. Witnessing her happiness and pride was an incredible experience, bringing joy to my heart.

Aadhya's mother asked me about my future plans, and I replied that I hadn't really thought about it yet. I was still trying to figure out what I wanted to do in life.

"Aadhya laughed and said, 'It's not true, mom. Atharv was just joking. He has different plans. Since he scored exceptionally well in his exams, he intends to pursue research work.

And she looked at me, acknowledging my words, and said, "Right, Atharv!"

I eagerly added, "Yes, yes, Auntie. In fact, I aspire to join ISRO And then her dad chimed in, saying, "So, have you also completed the application for the research college like Aadhya?" I replied, slightly taken aback, "No, I haven't."

Confused, I turned to Aadhya and asked, "Which research college, Aadhya? Uncle, what are you referring to?"

Aadhya's mother clarified, "Aadhya will be joining a research college in Bangalore for her undergraduate studies."

I turned towards Aadhya, my eyes silently questioning why she hadn't informed me about all of this beforehand.

It wasn't that I had an issue with her pursuing research in college. What left me feeling disappointed was the fact that she hadn't shared this information earlier. Had she informed me, I might have considered applying to the same college.

As Iti and Shreya arrived to congratulate Aadhya on her excellent marks, Iti exclaimed with excitement, "Oh, Atharv, what a surprise! You're here too!"

Responding with a somewhat unpleasant tone, I muttered, "Yeah."

Aadhya's mother interjected, announcing that it was time to eat. She kindly invited us to join them for a meal, but I politely declined, stating that I wasn't hungry. Iti and Shreya echoed my words, thanking Aadhya's mother for the invitation but also declining to eat.

Aadhya responded to her mother, saying, "Yes, mom, I'm not hungry either. You both have your food. I'll go to my room with my friends."

As soon as we entered the room, Iti couldn't contain her excitement and exclaimed, "Aadhya, did you tell your parents about Atharv? Oh my God, wow! This is such an amazing day!"

I interrupted Iti and said, "Aadhya didn't inform her parents about me. So, stop being happy. In fact, she didn't even inform me about her plans to go to Bangalore for her studies."

Aadhya chose to remain silent, and in her place, Shreya took it upon herself to speak up. She asserted, "If Aadhya did indeed secure admission, it would be more appropriate for you to offer her congratulations instead of reacting with anger."

Shreya's intervention in the conversation between Aadhya and me left me feeling upset and irritated. I had expected to have a direct dialogue with Aadhya, and Shreya's interference felt like an intrusion into our personal interaction. It seemed as though she was assuming a role that wasn't hers to play, and it disrupted the dynamic between Aadhya and me. I wished that Shreya had respected our conversation and allowed Aadhya to express her own thoughts and feelings.

In response to Shreya's interference, I expressed my frustration, telling her that her advice was unsolicited and it would be better if she refrained from speaking to me. I emphasized the importance of having a one-on-one conversation with Aadhya without any external interference.

Shreya, fueled by anger, retaliated and questioned my audacity to dismiss her and dictate her interactions with her friend. She defended Aadhya, implying that I had no right to scold or reprimand her.

Iti, trying to diffuse the tension between us, intervened and urged both Shreya and me to calm down. She reminded us that the focus should be on resolving the issue between Aadhya and me, rather than engaging in a conflict with each other.

Shreya, in a dramatic tone, asked Aadhya if she should leave, seemingly feigning concern and portraying herself as a caring friend.

Aadhya took a conciliatory approach and apologized on my behalf, assuring Shreya that she was welcome to stay. She also extended the invitation to Iti, suggesting that they all remain together despite the tense situation.

Upon hearing Aadhya's response, I attempted to clarify my position and express my concerns. I emphasized that my issue was not with Aadhya pursuing admission in the college but rather with not being informed about her decision beforehand. I explained that if she had informed me earlier, I would have tried to apply for admission in the same college. I also expressed my worries about the distance between us and how it would impact our ability to meet and spend time together.

Shreya continued to voice her opinions, accusing me of being mean and selfish. According to her, I was expecting Aadhya to sacrifice her dream college for the sake of our relationship. She criticized my self-centeredness, highlighting that Aadhya had already expressed her willingness to give up the opportunity, yet I was still thinking only about myself.

I reiterated my request to Shreya, firmly asking her to stop interpreting my words and to remain silent during the conversation between Aadhya and me. However, to my surprise and concern, Shreya responded with a declaration of her intent to engage in a confrontation or fight with me.

Overwhelmed by the situation, Aadhya's emotions spilled over, and she began to cry. Sensing the need to diffuse the tension, Iti stepped in, attempting to calm everyone involved. Reminding me of the advice shared during our farewell, Iti emphasized that my current actions were not aligned with what was suggested.

In that moment, I finally grasped that Shreya's behavior was consistent and predictable. It became evident that engaging in further arguments with her would only perpetuate the discord and exacerbate Aadhya's distress. Recognizing the importance of prioritizing Aadhya's emotional well-being, I realized that offering comfort and support was far more valuable than continuing to engage in futile disputes with Shreya.

I went to Aadhya and gently wiped away her tears, expressing my remorse. I said, "I'm sorry. It just saddens me a little when I realize you'll be far away from me. However, I am genuinely happy for you and your achievements."

I continued, "Alright, let me know when you plan to go there, and I will also start applying for admission in a private college in the same area. That way, we can still be closer to each other and support each other in our respective journeys."

Shreya said, 'There's no way this ghost will leave you alone,' and Aadhya put a finger on her lips in response.

Aadhya looked at me with a smile and asked, "And what about after that?"

I replied, "Well, after we study together and enjoy our time in Bangalore, we can explore the city, go to restaurants, watch movies, and even pursue jobs. And who knows, maybe in the future, we might even decide to get married."

Iti burst into laughter and exclaimed, "Then you should have kids there in Bangalore too!"

Aadhya's smile grew wider as she expressed her apology, saying, "Shut up, Iti! Atharv, I'm sorry, but I honestly didn't expect to pass that exam. I took it casually, and it was an online exam, which is why I didn't inform you earlier."

I reassured her, saying, "No problem at all. Besides, I also plan to take admission in a college in the same area, so we won't have any issues being together."

Aadhya firmly expressed her perspective, saying, "There's no need for you to go to such lengths. Besides, let's not forget what mom and dad discussed with you earlier. They emphasized the importance of prioritizing your personal goals and working towards achieving them. Once you have successfully accomplished your objectives, then you can approach them to ask for my hand in marriage. It's a straightforward and logical process based on our family's values."

Iti joyfully exclaimed, "Oh, how heartwarming and lovely!"

Shreya contemplated for a moment and replied, "Well, life is unpredictable

I smiled back at Shreya and nodded in agreement, saying, "Exactly, who knows what destiny has in store for us."

Turning to Aadhya, I said, "I'll give you a call later, Aadhya. Let's catch up soon." With that, I began making my way back home, carrying the memories of our conversation with me.

As I made my way out, my mind was consumed with the thought of how love turns us into great actors. It's as if we are playing a part in a movie, constantly pretending to be happy, even when we're not. It's a necessary act that we must put on, to keep the facade of our relationship afloat.

But deep down, the sadness lingers, eating away at us, until we forget what it's like to be truly happy.On the one hand, I was saddened by Adhya's departure to Bangalore, but on the other hand, I was also happy to hear that she had been accepted into her dream college." it's not wrong to say that

Sometimes Love can also make us selfish too. We want this person to stay with us, and only us, forever. We become possessive, jealous, and controlling, wanting to hold onto them with an iron grip. With a heavy heart, I returned home, and my mother greeted me, saying, 'Welcome home, let's get you cleaned up, and I'll prepare some food for you.'

I replied, 'I'll have my meal later in the night, I'm not hungry right now. Also, I'd like to have some time to myself, so could you please leave me alone in my room for a while?

My mother replied, 'There's no need to be sad. You have achieved excellent marks, unlike me when I was your age. I didn't perform as well as you did. I smiled and said, 'No, it's not about the marks. I just want to be alone for a while.' With that, I walked towards my room. She recognized my desire for some alone time and responded,

'No problem, just inform me if you feel hungry later.

As soon as I entered my room, I remembered a conversation I overheard between Adhya's parents regarding life goals.

As a science student, I had a plethora of options to explore in life. However, having too many choices can also lead to confusion and indecisiveness.

I decided to set aside all the thoughts and went to sleep as I realized that a fresh mind would be better for contemplating my future plans. I went to bed with this thought and fell asleep.

I woke up to the sound of laughter coming from outside my room. As I walked out, I saw my mother and Aadhya laughing about some mischievous incident from my childhood. My mother was sharing some of my childhood stories with Aadhya, and she was listening enthusiastically.

As I stepped outside, my mother noticed my presence and playfully remarked to Aadhya, highlighting my recent inclination to sleep excessively since the exams had ended. Aadhya joined the conversation, relating to my experience and sharing that she had also found herself sleeping more than usual after completing her exams.

Mom made a connection between Aadhya and me, emphasizing the similarity in our post-exam behavior. Recognizing our shared experiences, she encouraged us to engage in conversation while she kindly offered to make tea for us. With that, she headed towards the kitchen, leaving Aadhya and me to continue our conversation.

I was overjoyed that Aadhya had come to meet me and that she was so comfortable with my mother. This was a dream come true for me. Until now, only Shantanu used to come to my house in this manner. Seeing Aadhya, I was reminded of him and tears welled up in my eyes.

Aadhya said, "You look like a wild man! Go wash your face and come back here." I replied, "No, it's just that I met you a little while ago, and you are here. I hope you're not a dream." Aadhya laughed and said, "No, I'm not dream. That's why I told you to go wash your face."

"Could you please explain why you appeared so unexpectedly? Don't get me wrong, I'm genuinely glad to see you, but I must admit I'm also experiencing a sense of unease. Would you mind shedding some light on the situation? I'd appreciate it if you could help me understand."

"Aadhya mentioned that she would be traveling to Bangalore for document verification in just two days. It's been a rather quiet day between us, and earlier, you mentioned that you would give me a call once you arrived home, but I didn't hear from you. There are numerous matters I wanted to discuss with you, which is why I find myself here now."

I said with exhaustion evident in my voice, "Oh yeah, I was so tired when I reached home that I fell asleep."And then I was planning to call you, but I couldn't get around to it. It's great that you're going to Bangalore for document verification.Trying to push my own emotions aside, I added, "You informed me so soon, and I'm genuinely happy for you," though a trace of sadness remained in my eyes.

Aadhya said that she knew that I wouldn't like it , that's why she wanted to come and tell me herself. She had planned everything, but then she was called to school, and suddenly Shreya and Iti also came there.

Feeling a sense of annoyance, I voiced my discontent. "If your intention was to have a conversation with me, you should have asked them to leave. And I strongly urge you not to mention Shreya again. It seemed like you were taking her side previously, and now you want to discuss her?!"

Aadhya noticed my anger and said, "Atharv, you're getting so angry all of a sudden. I understand that I made a mistake by not informing you about my exam and admission earlier. However, please believe that my intention was solely to surprise you, and I genuinely had no expectation of being admitted there myself.

After observing my silence, Aadhya continued, "Let's not dwell on the past any longer. The main reason I came here today is to let you know that I genuinely agree with your earlier suggestion of going for lunch tomorrow at a restaurant. It's an opportunity for us to spend some quality time together and enjoy a good meal. I hope you'll consider it and we can move forward from this misunderstanding."

I took a deep breath and nodded. "You're right, sorry for getting so worked up. Let's talk and clear things out. And I'd love to have lunch with you tomorrow.

We decided on a restaurant and made plans to meet there the next day for lunch. As Aadhya left, I realized how important it was to communicate properly and not let anger get in the way of relationships.

We sometimes waste our precious moments on small things that have no connection to our relationships. For instance, let's say Aadhya's friend didn't like me and I didn't like her either, but because of all the issues between them, it was Aadhya who was suffering. Fighting with Aadhya about her friend was like putting a dent in our relationship, which was a small thing but still taking up our time.

As Aadhya left, my mother came and said, "Oh, I made tea and where did Aadhya go?" I replied, "She went back to her house. She remembered some work she had to do." My mother then said, "This girl is so sweet. Talking to her made me feel like I found my own daughter."

I said, "Why do you get so emotional? It's okay, she just went back to her own home. But you know what? Your son is better than her. My mom said, "I will pray to God that she finds a guy who is even better than you in her life.I said, "Mom, there's no need to pray for that.

Aadhya is a smart girl, and I have faith that she will find someone who is perfect for her. It's not about finding someone better or worse, it's about finding someone who is right for her and makes her happy. My mom smiled, and her smile was enough to indicate that she had found the answer she was looking for.

In the evening, my father summoned me to his room and shared, "I have shortlisted three colleges for you, and their exam forms are now available. Make sure you fill them out promptly so that you can secure admission as soon as possible." Reflecting on the passage of time, he added, "It's hard to believe how swiftly children grow up. It feels like only yesterday I was getting your admission done in school, and now you're on the verge of entering college. My son is growing up."

Curious about my father's words, I inquired, "Why are you saying this?" He replied, his voice tinged with emotion, "When you become a father yourself one day, you will understand this feeling. We tirelessly strive for the well-being of our loved ones, but often find ourselves lacking the time to truly be with them, sit with them, or engage in heartfelt conversations." Taking a moment to compose himself, he then added, "Come on, get up and fill out these forms."

As I stepped into my room, my father's words lingered in my mind. They weighed heavily on my heart, tugging at a deeply buried guilt I had not realized existed. In that moment, I found myself contemplating the truth of his words, realizing just how much of my life I had taken for granted.

As I pondered my father's words, my thoughts drifted towards my mother and the deep connection I shared with her. The countless moments of laughter, warm hugs, and heartfelt stories we shared were abundant in my memory. However, when it came to my father, our interactions seemed to revolve primarily around practical matters such as paying fees or requesting gifts. Our relationship seemed driven by necessity rather than genuine affection. This realization left me contemplating the depth and nature of our bond, wondering if there was room for a deeper connection to be nurtured.

As I sat there, consumed by my thoughts, a profound realization struck me. I couldn't recall the last time I expressed my love to my father or simply engaged in a heartfelt conversation with him about life. A profound wave of regret and sorrow washed over me, realizing that I had unintentionally taken for granted the love and care of one of the most significant individuals in my life.

But as the evening wore on and I filled out the exam forms for the colleges my father had shortlisted, I began to understand the gravity of his words. He had been right all along. The bond between a father and son was something special, something to be cherished and nurtured. And I realized that it was up to me to do just that, to show my father just how much he meant to me.

As I handed in the forms, I turned to my father with a renewed sense of love and appreciation. I hugged him tightly, the words "I love you, Dad" spilling out of my mouth before I could even think about them. And as he hugged me back, tears streaming down his face .

My father's voice trembled with emotion; he quickly cleared his throat and said, "Come on now, don't be silly. Let's not cry anymore. Look at the admission forms and fill them out. Time is running out." I could tell that he was attempting to lift the mood, but his words only served to pull at my heartstrings even more. His unwavering love and concern for me flooded my senses, and I couldn't help but feel an intense gratitude for having such a caring father.

The next day, I went to the shop to find a gift for Aadhya before meeting her for lunch. I wanted to give her something special and memorable. Even though she had never asked me for anything, I had seen in movies that giving gifts is a way to show someone you care about them, so I decided to do just that.

As I browsed through the store, I finally found a musical couple toy that danced together. It was perfect! But when I asked the shopkeeper about the price, he quoted a whopping 1700 rupees, which was way beyond my budget. If I spent all my money on the gift, I wouldn't have anything left for our lunch.

I felt disappointed and helpless. I really wanted to buy the gift for Aadhya, but I couldn't afford it. Finally, I made the tough decision to leave the toy and continue searching for something else.

The shopkeeper asked me, "Should I pack this one or show you something else?" Then, someone spoke in a loud voice, "Brother, you are quoting a higher price. Okay, let's settle on a reasonable price for this toy and when I turned back to look, it was Iti.I asked, "Hey, what are you doing here? Why do you keep following me around? It feels like you're spying on me." Iti chuckled and replied, "Oh, what's the matter? This shop is actually ours by mistake, and he is my brother. I came here to deliver their lunch box, so don't worry, you're not under any surveillance

As we stood in the shop, the shopkeeper grinned at Iti and exclaimed, "This young lady is always spoiling my business. She comes here and disrupts everything." Iti turned to me and informed me that the price of the toy we were eyeing was 570 rupees. "Do you have enough money for it, or should I pitch in with you?" she asked. At first, I was taken aback by her generosity, but then I chuckled and replied, "Don't worry, I have that much with me.

Iti made a funny face and said to the shopkeeper, "Hello, pack this gift and don't make a big deal out of it. He's my brother too, and I know he came to buy this gift for Aadhya.That shopkeeper smiled and said, "Okay, fine.

I thanked Iti and requested her not to tell Aadhya about the gift. She agreed and advised me to take care of Aadhya because she was not an easy-going girl but a stubborn one who used to do things her own way. It was me who had done some magic on her and now she had changed completely.I said, "I will try, but did I do something wrong? I mean, I didn't tell her to change, and I don't even know how she was before." Iti laughed and said, "Atharv, you are so innocent bro. Just forget about it. She then bid me farewell and I expressed my gratitude once again for the discount. She responded, "No problem," which brought a smile to my face.

After saying goodbye to Iti, I arrived home and carefully stored the gift. When my mom called me to have lunch, I told her I was going out to eat with a friend, without disclosing the friend's name. Even though my mom wouldn't get angry upon hearing Aadhya's name, there was still a sense of hesitation or certain level of relationship one has with their parents, despite their understanding nature. One needs to maintain a sense of respect and decorum because you can't simply say that you're going out to eat with your girlfriend or a female friend

Mom responded, "Okay, you can go. By the way, some of my friends are coming over, and we're having a kitty party today." I chuckle and respond, "Sure, Mom, you go ahead with your kirtan party. I remember how Mrs. Sharma sings devotional songs and Mrs. Gupta dances to them. And then you all enjoy the prasad and give fake compliments to each other.

My mom's response was filled with anger as she warned me, "You're talking too much. After sharing a laugh with my mom, I left home.

Motivated to avoid repeating my previous mistake of being late, I took the initiative to call Aadhya and confirm her expected arrival time. She promptly informed me that she would be there in just five minutes. Filled with a renewed sense of urgency, I accelerated my bike and set off on my way. However, as I rode, a sinking feeling washed over me as I realized that in the rush, I had forgotten to bring the gift I had intended to give her.

Frustrated, I mentally berated myself, "Hey brain, how could you be so foolish? You couldn't remember until I was already leaving the house, and now, when I'm almost there, you remind me that the gift is still at home. What am I supposed to do now?" Despite my internal pleas, my brain seemed stubbornly unresponsive. Overwhelmed with anger towards myself, I reluctantly turned back towards home, realizing that retrieving the gift was the only option left.

Well do you know? What's the difference between crazy people and introverted people? It's just that one talks to themselves out loud, and the other talks to themselves inside their head always.

As I reached home and opened the gate, I saw that the kitty(kirtan) party was going on. Mrs. Gupta was dancing, and Mrs. Sharma was singing devotional songs. I didn't feel like laughing this time, and I was getting late too. So, I quickly took the gift and left.

On the way, I began contemplating the life of housewives. They are occupied with household chores from dawn until dusk, and their contribution to the family often goes unnoticed until their health starts to decline. Perhaps, that is why they arranged this kitty party - as a means of taking a short break and unwinding from their daily routine.

So, lost in my thoughts, I arrived at the restaurant and all I could think was that I had made Aadhya wait for me again.I saw Aadhya and apologized, telling her that I was late because I was getting her a gift. She smiled and said, "It's okay, there must be a reason why you were late.

"I am grateful for her understanding of nature. Despite my tardiness, she didn't seem upset at all. Instead, she radiated positivity and warmth, as she always did. I admire her for it and asked her how she always managed to stay so positive." She simply shrugged and said, "Life is too short to dwell on the negatives. There's always a reason why things happen, and we just need to trust that everything will work out in the end."Her words struck a chord with me.

I asked Aadhya if she reads novels or where she gets all these good thoughts from. She replied, "In novels, there's also a person who writes it, and these things come with time and experience. It's part of our nature. And if I have any good qualities, it's because of my grandmother.

I said "Grandmother" and then I asked, "Does your grandmother have a hand in the color changes of your eyes too?" To which she replied, "No, no, why do you think my eyes change color because of my grandmother? Look again, what do you see in this? And when I looked, it seemed as though there wasn't just a color, but there was a sparkle in her eyes today. I said, "Wow, it's like you do magic, your eyes seem to shine like a torch is being lit!

Aadhya blushed and asked me about the gift I had brought. She teased me about using my parents' money to buy her gifts and said that I should wait until I earned money on my own before giving her any more gifts. Despite her playful teasing, I knew that she appreciated the thought behind the gift and the effort I had put into it.

As I nodded in agreement, the waiter arrived to take our order. We ordered two veg thalis and waited for our food to arrive. While we waited, I asked Aadhya if she was always like this or if she had changed over time. Aadhya replied, "No. I used to be very weird earlier. Since childhood, I used to compete with others, be it in getting good grades or dressing up better. If someone scored better than me or wore nicer clothes, I had to do the same.

In fact, I changed after I called you a monkey for the first time. It made me feel bad and before that, I had never thought so much about anyone else. But as I kept talking to you, all this stubbornness and competition with others just disappeared. After meeting you, it feels like I can just stop and be content. You don't even know how happy I am to have lunch with you today. It's bringing me more joy than being the first in something.

After hearing all this, I couldn't help but feel blessed with her words. I said, "Aadhya, I'm sorry if I ever said anything hurtful to you in anger. And to be honest, it's not you who is lucky, it's me who is lucky to have you in my life.

Aadhya reassured me, saying, "No, there's no need to apologize. We have a beautiful present and future ahead of us." I nodded in agreement, a smile spreading across my face, and replied, "Yes, absolutely." Just then, our thalis arrived, marking the beginning of our meal together.

We enjoyed our meal together. And then Aadhya said, 'Listen, I have also brought something for you, but it's not like a gift.' I replied, 'No problem, tell me what you have brought.' She then took out a neem leaf and some mishri (crystallized sugar) from her purse.

Curiously, I posed an intriguing question, "Hey, what have you brought? It looks like a neem leaf to me." Is it the same?' She replied, 'Yes, it is.' Then I asked, 'Are you suggesting that we should also eat it after our lunch?' She exclaimed, 'Wow, how do you know this?

I reiterated, "No, I can't eat it. It has a very bitter taste." Aadhya reassured me, "Okay, no problem. I'll eat it first, and then you don't have to worry about it." I still had my reservations and questioned, "Is it really necessary to eat it? Besides, you shouldn't eat it either."

"This food is so delicious, and if we eat the neem leaf, won't it ruin the taste?" Aadhya nodded in agreement, acknowledging the potential impact on the overall flavor. However, her face momentarily reflected sadness. Sensing her disappointment, I reconsidered and said, "Okay, bring it, and let me give it a try." Taking a leap of faith, I placed the neem leaf in my mouth, fully aware of its bitter taste. Aadhya encouraged me, saying, "Now, chew it." Despite the strong bitterness, I embraced the experience, knowing it was my only option at that moment. Aadhya then handed me some mishri, a sweet treat, to help balance out the intense flavor.

With a smile, Aadhya expressed her gratitude by saying, "Thank you." Intrigued by the experience, I couldn't help but inquire, "What was that all about? Could you please explain the reasoning behind it?"

Aadhya proceeded to provide an insightful explanation, saying, "In our culture, whenever we embark on something new, such as starting a new school or business, we follow this ritual. It has been passed down by my grandmother.

According to her, life presents us with moments that can be likened to neem leaves and mishri. The idea is that you must consume the neem leaf, which represents bitterness, before indulging in the sweetness of the mishri. By doing so, you gain a deeper appreciation for the sweetness that follows, and it serves as a reminder that in life, we may encounter hardships or challenges before we can truly savor the joys and sweetness that lie ahead."

After seeing my confused face, Aadhya said, look in our life, if we work hard now, we will achieve success in the future. But if we have fun now, life may become difficult later.

Curious and slightly skeptical, I questioned Aadhya further, asking, "Was it really necessary to go through this activity? Couldn't you have simply told me about it without going through the ritual? Or did your research on this start just now?" Aadhya burst into uncontrollable laughter and replied, "Atharv, that's the whole point of the ritual. If I hadn't done it practically, you would have forgotten it later. I smiled back. And nodded in understanding and thanked Aadhya for sharing this beautiful tradition with me.

It made me realize how important it is to cherish and appreciate both the bitter and sweet moments in life. We finished our lunch and continued our conversation, talking about our future plans and aspirations. It was a wonderful day, and I felt grateful to have such a thoughtful and caring girl like Aadhya in my life.

And then I called the waiter to ask for the bill. Suddenly, Aadhya also took out her wallet, and I thought she was going to take out another neem leaf. But then she said, "Let's split the bill. We'll contribute equally since we both had our meal. I said, "It's okay, next time you can pay," but Aadhya insisted, and even suggested that on the day I earn, she will let me pay. And then I noticed the girl who won the debate competition inside her. You cannot argue in front of her, nor can you prove her logic wrong. I also learned this. It was the first time we had spent so much time together like this, and as we know, every moment has a limit, and that moment had come to an end.

As we left the restaurant, Aadhya gently took hold of my hand and made a heartfelt request, saying, "Promise me that you will study well in college and wholeheartedly focus on building your career." I replied without hesitation, "Yes, absolutely." Our eyes met, and she continued with a serious tone, "And also, please avoid getting involved with any other girl." Her words carried a sense of protectiveness and a desire to ensure our bond remained strong.

Amused by Aadhya's remark, I chuckled and playfully responded, "Don't worry, this monkey has found his tree, and I'll focus on my career too. But don't give me that look, or I might not let you leave." Aadhya laughed along and replied, "All right, all right. I'm going now. Bye, take care." With those parting words, she left, leaving me with a mix of lightheartedness and fondness for our playful banter. I watched her disappear into the crowd before making my way back home, lost in thought about the day's events.

As I feel grateful for the time I spent with Aadhya. She had taught me so much in just a few short hours.

Aadhya completely changed my outlook on love. I realized that it wasn't just the clichéd version of boy-meets-girl, where they exchange gifts, go on romantic dates, and eventually get married. It was so much more than that. Aadhya had taught me that love was about supporting each other, working hard towards our goals, and cherishing the moments we spent together.

Her gift of neem and mishri was not just a gesture of love, but also a symbol of her unwavering support for my future aspirations. She had shown me that love was not just about grand gestures, but also about the little things that showed how much we cared for each other.

After returning home with a sense of joy, I quickly washed my hands and face before settling into my room to call out for my mother. Despite making multiple attempts to get her attention, she remained engrossed in her book. Frustrated, I made my way to her room and found her reading with a smile on her face.

I stood in front of her and questioned, "I have been calling out to you for a while now. Why aren't you listening?" She glanced at me briefly, but then continued reading, paying no attention to my words.

I persisted in my attempt to understand the situation and asked my mom, "Mom, what happened? Why aren't you talking to me?" Her response was curt and distant as she replied, "Don't disturb me. I am reading my book." It was at that moment I realized that she was still upset about the joke I had made earlier, and her silence spoke volumes about her lingering displeasure.

I immediately apologized, saying, "No, no, I was just joking. I didn't mean to hurt you so much." I felt remorse for my actions and hoped to make amends with my mother.

But she was still ignoring me and reading her book. I asked, "Okay, tell me what are you reading that's making you laugh so much?" She replied, "I am reading the stories of Lord Krishna and Mother Yashoda.

In response to my mom's distant behavior, I attempted to lighten the mood by sharing a comparison, saying, "You know, even Lord Krishna used to trouble his mother." She then closed her book and issued a warning, stating that if I ever mentioned her friends or her kitty party again, she would discipline me. I laughed and quickly apologized, saying, "Okay, okay, sorry."

Sensing my mom's change of heart, she asked if I wanted her to make tea for me, to which I gladly accepted her offer by saying, "Yes, please."

I realized that perhaps she was really hurt by what I said. That small party meant a lot to her where she used to sit with her friends and gossip.

I also noticed that it is relatively easy to appease our mother when she is upset with us, and this relationship is not like any other. Here, all it takes is a heartfelt apology to make things right, and sometimes she forgives us even if we don't admit our mistakes.

As I sat there, eagerly awaiting my tea, I noticed my father returning home from work. Spotting me, he asked if I had completed the form, to which I nodded in affirmation. Filled with enthusiasm, I began recounting the story of how I had playfully teased my mother earlier in the day, eager to share the lighthearted moment with my father.

My father chuckled and remarked, "We should avoid mocking women for their TV serials and gossip." Intrigued, I questioned him as to why this was the case. My father shrugged and speculated, "Perhaps, after marriage, women often drift apart from many of their old acquaintances. As a result, these TV serials and local gossip sessions serve as their new companions in a unique way."

Then, I asked if this phenomenon also applied to girls, to which he replied that it may indeed apply to them as well. He added that if he had a daughter, he would probably be more aware of such things. He suggested that I should ask my mother this question to get a better understanding of her perspective. I smiled and replied, "No, she might get angry with me again." My father and I both chuckled, enjoying the moment of levity.

A few days had passed since I had submitted my college applications, and I was anxiously awaiting any news about my admissions status. To my delight, I received a phone call from a college in Delhi, informing me that I had been selected for admission.

The college representative requested that I bring my documents to their campus in order to complete the admission process. Excited and eager to take advantage of this opportunity, I immediately informed my father of the good news.

Despite the considerable distance between Delhi and our hometown, both my father and I were resolute in our decision to undertake the journey for my college admission. The following morning, we rose early, ensuring that all my necessary documents were prepared and ready. With a sense of determination, we set off on the long road trip, eager to reach our destination and begin this new chapter of my academic journey.

During our travel, a whirlwind of emotions enveloped me, blending excitement and nervousness together. I was fully aware that this moment marked a significant milestone in my life, and the thought of attending college in Delhi evoked both thrilling anticipation and a touch of apprehension.

Until now, my knowledge of the city was mostly derived from televised broadcasts of the grand Republic Day celebrations held in Delhi. I had also heard about the existence of the efficient Delhi Metro system and the concerns regarding crime rates in certain areas. However, despite these tidbits of information, I lacked a comprehensive understanding of what the city truly had in store for me.

As I entered Delhi, my mind conjured up vivid images of cabinet ministers engaged in important meetings and iconic landmarks such as the majestic Red Fort and the towering Qutub Minar. However, my initial impressions of the city were shaped by the reality of heavy traffic and the maze-like network of narrow, winding roads that seemed to stretch out endlessly before me.

Despite my preconceived notions of Delhi as a grand, official-looking city, I found that it was difficult to differentiate it from other bustling metropolises. The buildings and streets were not immediately distinguishable as the capital of India. Instead, the traffic and chaos of the city dominated my first impressions.

After navigating through the heavy traffic, my father and I finally arrived at the college. A security guard directed us to the block where admissions were being processed. The college was quite large, and we found ourselves struggling to make our way from one block to another.

As we arrived at the admission office, the first question posed to us was which stream we were seeking admission to. It was clear that this was a critical decision, as it would impact our entire academic journey at the college. We carefully considered our options before deciding on the stream that we felt would best align with our interests and aspirations.

To be honest, I had not made a decision about which stream to choose before arriving at the college. My admission had been accepted in three different streams, so when the admission officer asked me which one I wanted to pursue, I made a spontaneous decision and chose computer science. It was the subject that I felt most interested in and confident about, given its relevance in today's digital world.

Whenever I hear or read about computers, it always reminds me of a story from my childhood that my mother used to tell me. The story was about how the USA had refused to sell a supercomputer to India, but Indian scientists persevered and went on to build their own computer within the country.

And after the admission was confirmed, my father called home to inform my mother about it.

As I communicated with Aadhya about my admission, she promptly called me back, expressing her happiness and congratulating me. She also shared that she had been allotted a hostel and had some pending college formalities to complete before the classes started. Unfortunately, she couldn't come home to meet me due to her commitments.

When my father heard me talking on the phone, he reminded me in a commanding tone to hurry up and come home quickly, emphasizing the need to be punctual. Sensing his urgency, I quickly ended the call with Aadhya, bidding her farewell, and acknowledging that we would talk later.

With my father's reminder lingering in my mind, I focused on wrapping up my tasks and making my way back home.

When I arrived home, my mother expressed her concern about my decision to study in Delhi and questioned if it was necessary for me to go so far away for my education. She became emotional and started crying, worrying about how I would manage in a new city and expressing her fear that I might feel scared or lonely.

In an attempt to reassure her, my father intervened and explained that there was a nearby hostel where I would have all the necessary facilities and support. However, my mother insisted on speaking directly with me to inquire further.

I reassured my mother confidently, telling her that I wouldn't be afraid and that I was ready to face the challenges that lay ahead. In response, my mother made me promise that if I encountered any difficulties or felt overwhelmed, I would immediately inform her by giving her a call.

After our conversation, my mother seemed reassured and began preparing for my journey to college. She packed my belongings, including clothes, books, and other essentials. But what surprised me was the additional items she packed, such as a variety of biscuits and savories. It felt as though she was preparing me for a battle instead of just going to study in college. Nonetheless, I appreciated her loving gesture and understood that it was her way of ensuring I had everything I needed.

Once the packing was complete, we embarked on our journey back to Delhi. Upon reaching the city, my mother introduced me to some of our relatives who lived nearby. She took the initiative to save their phone numbers in my phone, emphasizing the importance of staying connected with family and having a support system.

My father also made sure that I had a local SIM card, so I wouldn't have to worry about roaming charges while staying in Delhi. It was a thoughtful gesture that showed his commitment to my convenience and safety.

Finally, we reached the hostel, and together we unloaded all my belongings and settled them into my room. The moment of farewell arrived, and both my father and mother smiled at me, wishing me the best for my new college life. Their love and support were palpable, and it gave me the confidence to embark on this new chapter with enthusiasm and determination.

5

The Surprise Visit

As I stepped into the hostel, a wave of nostalgia crashed over me, reminding me of the poignant moments from the movie "Taare Zameen Par." The scene where young Ishaan is left sobbing by his parents at boarding school resonated deeply within me, despite my being older than him. I couldn't shake off the overwhelming sensation of venturing into uncharted territory, leaving behind the comfort of my home for the first time.

Surveying my new surroundings, I felt like an outsider in an unfamiliar realm. Though the faces around me bore a resemblance to mine, I found myself surrounded by strangers. It was as if I had been transported to an entirely different planet, struggling to find my footing and establish a sense of belonging in this new world.

I took a moment to gather my thoughts and reminded myself that I had embarked on this journey with a purpose.

I eventually located my assigned room, my heart pounding as I entered. Two boys who had already settled into the space greeted me warmly, which helped to ease my anxiety somewhat. However, the reality of the situation hit me hard. This was a triple-seater room because all the double-seaters were taken, and the one-seaters were reserved for third and fourth-year students.

Despite my roommates' welcoming attitude, the space felt cramped for three people.

I stepped out of my room and dialed Aadhya's number. As she answered the phone, her voice filled me with a sense of familiarity and comfort. She asked if it was me speaking, and I confirmed, relieved to hear her voice on the other end. I proceeded to share my new contact number with her.

With a hint of longing in my voice, I began to explain my current room situation. I mentioned that I had been assigned to a shared room, where I would be living with other residents. The realization that I would no longer have the privacy and familiarity of my own space sank in, and I couldn't help but express that I was already missing home.

Aadhya listened attentively, understanding the mix of emotions I was experiencing. She empathized with my situation, acknowledging that it was natural to feel a sense of longing for the comfort and familiarity of home, especially in such a new and unfamiliar environment. She assured me that it was okay to miss home and that it would take time to adjust to the changes.

In her soothing voice, Aadhya reminded me that this shared room was an opportunity to meet new people and build connections. She encouraged me to reach out to my roommates, engage in conversations, and find common ground. Aadhya emphasized that while it might be challenging at first, establishing a sense of camaraderie with those around me could ease the feelings of homesickness and make the hostel experience more enriching.

Upon hearing Aadhya's reassuring words, I found solace in knowing that she had experienced similar feelings when she first arrived at the hostel. Her ability to adjust herself to the new environment gave me hope that I too could overcome these initial challenges.

Taking Aadhya's advice to heart, I realized the importance of spending time with my roommates. Just as they were unknown to me, I was also unknown to them. By immersing myself in their company and engaging in conversations, I could begin to forge connections and foster a sense of belonging.

In an attempt to alleviate my longing for companionship, I suggested to Aadhya that she should talk to me more frequently, as her presence would provide me comfort. However, she chuckled and gently reminded me that relying solely on her would hinder my ability to understand society and gain confidence in navigating life's challenges. Her words resonated with me, making me realize the importance of developing my own social skills and finding my place in the broader world.

Aadhya further encouraged me by asking how long I intended to confine myself within the closed walls of my room. Her question served as a gentle push, reminding me that isolating myself would only prolong my adjustment period. She advised me to gather my courage and rejoin my roommates, actively participating in the hostel community.

Realizing the validity of Aadhya's guidance, I replied, "Okay, we will talk every day." Her agreement filled me with a sense of warmth and reassurance, knowing that I could count on her support and friendship even as I ventured out to make new connections.

Feeling motivated by my conversation with Aadhya, I entered the room where the two guys were engaged in conversation. One of them, Vivhan, noticed my presence and kindly invited me to join them. He immediately sensed my shyness and inquired about the reason behind it, encouraging me to open up.

With a warm smile, Vivhan stretched his hand out in a gesture of friendship, introducing himself. I reciprocated the gesture, shaking his hand firmly, and shared my name, Atharv. It felt reassuring to take this step forward, embracing the opportunity to connect with my roommates.

Eager to get to know everyone, I turned to the other guy in the room and politely asked for his name. Anvit seemed to mirror my initial shyness, but gradually, he mustered the courage to extend his hand. As he introduced himself, I listened attentively, appreciating his effort to break the ice.

As I interacted with Anvit, I couldn't help but notice his endearing demeanor, which reminded me of a young eighth-grade student stepping into college for the first time. His innocence and youthful charm evoked a sense of fondness within me, nurturing a brotherly affection towards him.

Curiosity sparked, I inquired about Anvit's hometown, wanting to learn more about his background and the place he called home. With a gentle smile, he shared that he hailed from Uttarakhand, a state known for its scenic beauty nestled in the foothills of the Himalayas.

His response piqued my interest, and I expressed my fascination with Uttarakhand, mentioning how I had heard about its breathtaking landscapes and rich cultural heritage. Anvit's eyes lit up, and he eagerly began to share anecdotes and stories about his hometown, painting vivid pictures with his words.

As he spoke passionately about the mountains, rivers, and vibrant traditions of Uttarakhand, I found myself captivated by his enthusiasm. It was clear that his connection to his homeland ran deep, and I felt a sense of awe and admiration for the place that had shaped him.

Vivhan made a suggestion that we should go and have dinner together and also take a tour of the college. Despite the fact that I had only met Vivhan ten minutes ago, I decided not to refuse his offer. So, the three of us embarked on a journey to explore the college campus. After stepping out, we leisurely wandered around the college, carefully examining and discovering every nook and cranny of the campus.

There were multiple hostels available for both boys and girls, lined up to the left of our own hostel. Each hostel had its own mess, and additional amenities such as ATMs were also provided. The college environment resembled a small city, with minimal traffic noise and students commuting on bicycles.

After a while, Anvit suggested that it was time for us to return as we had been exploring for quite some time. He mentioned the importance of getting some rest, considering we had orientation scheduled for the following day. I readily agreed to accompany him back to our hostel.

As we were about to enter our hostel, we noticed two guys standing outside our room. They didn't seem like students and appeared more like some sort of hooligans .

I approached the two guys standing outside our room and asked them if it was indeed our room. In a playful manner, they responded by exaggeratingly claiming that not only was the room ours, but the entire hostel and college belonged to us as well.

I chose not to engage in an argument with them and quietly proceeded towards my room. However, to my surprise, one of the guys grabbed me from behind and insisted on getting an introduction from me. This unexpected intrusion irritated me, and I questioned why I should provide my introduction without even knowing who they were. Just as the situation was escalating, Vivhan stepped in and proposed that they interview him first before I shared any personal information.

The two guys playfully teased Vivhan by pulling his ears, accusing him of being overly smart. They clarified that they were senior students in the hostel and it was a tradition for juniors to introduce themselves first. Considering the numerous questions we had asked them, they extended an invitation for us to join them in the hostel canteen, where other seniors were also conducting introductory sessions with their juniors.

Anvit glared at me, clearly frustrated, and sarcastically remarked, "Atharv, thanks to you, we ended up getting stuck here for no reason."

We followed our two senior companions to the canteen and noticed that there were already three guys seated at a table, engrossed in introducing themselves to their junior.

As soon as the three seniors spotted us, they called Anvit over and ordered him to introduce himself first. Anvit shared some personal details, including the fact that he had lost his mother, which led to an emotional response from both the seniors and us. However, Anvit managed to lighten the mood by mentioning his girlfriend, which made everyone laugh.

Next, it was Vivhan's turn to introduce himself, and he displayed such candor and openness with the seniors that it felt as if he was introducing himself to old friends. Impressed by his genuineness, the seniors willingly shared their phone numbers with Vivhan, urging him to reach out to them if we ever needed any assistance. They went on to assure us that they weren't as intimidating as they may seem and that their intention was simply to alleviate any fears we might have had.

Then, the attention turned to me as the seniors inquired about my name and field of study. When I mentioned that I was studying computer science, they chuckled mischievously and playfully challenged me to create a computer using only a piece of paper. Although it was a lighthearted request, I decided to take up the challenge and proceeded to draw a basic representation of a computer. This unexpected response from me amused the seniors even further, causing them to burst into laughter.

The seniors continued to encourage the three of us to build a stronger connection with them, emphasizing that we should reach out to them first in case of any problems or concerns, whether it involved attendance, project purchases, or any other challenges we might face. They reassured us that they were always available to assist us and advised us to feel free to call them anytime we needed help.

Expressing our gratitude, we thanked the seniors for their kindness and guidance. Upon returning to our room, we each selected our preferred beds and took the time to organize our closets, settling in and making ourselves comfortable in our new living space.

The following morning, filled with anticipation, we eagerly awaited the class schedule after the uneventful orientation. As soon as we received it, I quickly made my way back to our hostel room, eager to review it in detail. To my satisfaction, the schedule appeared to be well-balanced, offering a mix of theoretical and practical classes. Some days had multiple sessions lined up consecutively, while others allowed for more breaks in between. I was pleased to see that the lab schedules were strategically interspersed between the theoretical classes. This thoughtful arrangement would undoubtedly help us manage our time effectively and make the most of our learning opportunities.

After lunch, we huddled in our room, discussing our schedules and strategizing how best to tackle the challenges ahead. We agreed that we needed a break from the monotony of our room and decided to explore the hostel and its surroundings. As we walked around, we stumbled upon a small garden within the hostel complex. It was a serene oasis of calm amidst the hustle and bustle of college life.

The garden was a hidden gem, and we spent some time there, soaking in the peaceful surroundings. We admired the neatly trimmed hedges, the colorful flowers, and the towering trees that provided much-needed shade from the sun. The chirping of the birds and the rustling of the leaves were the only sounds we could hear.

As Aadhya had predicted, the three of us were slowly becoming good friends, and our seniors were guiding us to avoid the mistakes they had made. With their blessings, we felt confident and motivated to make the most of our time at the college. They not only helped us with our studies but also showed us around the campus and nearby areas, sharing interesting facts and stories about the college and its history. They even introduced us to some of their friends and encouraged us to participate in extracurricular activities.

It wasn't long before we became familiar faces around the college, and our seniors were proud to see us adapting well to the new environment. We would often meet up with them in the canteen or the garden and discuss our progress and challenges. They would share their experiences and offer suggestions on how to overcome any obstacles we were facing. We were grateful to have such supportive and caring seniors, who went out of their way to help us in any way they could.

As time passed, we realized that we had not only gained valuable knowledge but also lifelong friendships. Our seniors had become our mentors, and we had become their mentees. We were now part of a community, where everyone supported and looked out for each other. Our journey in college had just begun, but with the guidance and blessings of our seniors, we were ready to take on whatever challenges lay ahead.

Indeed, college is often a place where competition is palpable among students, even if it is not always visible on the surface. Each student brings their own unique set of talents and abilities to the table, whether it be in the realm of poetry, coding, dancing, or playing musical instruments.

Some students may possess a natural flair for crafting beautiful verses, expressing themselves through the power of words. Others may demonstrate exceptional skills in coding and programming, harnessing the power of technology to create innovative solutions. There are those who shine on the stage, captivating audiences with their dancing prowess, while others mesmerize with their musical talents, effortlessly playing instruments with skill and precision.

In this diverse environment, students are constantly inspired and motivated by the talents and achievements of their peers. While healthy competition exists, it often acts as a catalyst for personal growth and serves as a driving force for individuals to discover and develop their own unique abilities.

It became clear to us in the first semester that college life was bringing about a lot of changes within us. It was a place where we could explore our passions and develop new ones. We were constantly inspired by our peers and motivated to push ourselves further. The environment of healthy competition helped us to grow both academically and personally. It was a place where we learned to appreciate diversity and embrace the unique talents and abilities of each individual.

Despite having different college schedules, Aadhya and I found it challenging to have regular conversations, as we could only manage to talk two to three times a week. It wasn't because she was angry with me; rather, her workload made it difficult for her to find free time for chats. We both recognized the importance of maintaining our relationship and decided to come up with a solution.

Surprisingly, it was Aadhya who took the initiative and suggested creating a schedule for our conversations. She was naturally organized and understood the value of staying connected even amidst our busy lives. Together, we devised a plan where we would set aside a specific time each week to have uninterrupted conversations.

This arrangement allowed us to have dedicated and focused communication, ensuring that we could catch up, share our experiences, and support each other. Aadhya's proactive approach and commitment to our relationship demonstrated her genuine care and effort in making it work despite the challenges we faced.

By implementing this schedule, we found a way to maintain our connection and strengthen our bond, even in the midst of our demanding college lives. It served as a reminder of the importance of prioritizing and nurturing relationships, regardless of the constraints posed by our individual schedules.

However, I still made sure to speak with my mom every day to keep my family close to my heart.

One day, when I returned to my room after speaking with my mom, I noticed something strange. Anvit had broken a mirror and written names on two pieces and started talking in them.

Initially, I assumed that Anvit was joking or engaging in some form of playful activity. However, as he continued talking into the broken mirror pieces for a prolonged period of five to ten minutes, my concern grew. Recognizing the urgency of the situation, I hurriedly made my way to the basketball ground where Vivhan was playing and informed him about what was happening.

Without wasting a moment, Vivhan and I rushed back to our room. To my surprise, even upon seeing us enter the room, Anvit persisted in his actions, seemingly oblivious to our presence. The intensity of his engagement with the mirror pieces was disconcerting.

Suddenly, after a while, Anvit let out a loud shout of affirmation, exclaiming, "Yes!" The outburst startled both Vivhan and me, leaving us perplexed and unsure of what exactly had transpired.

Vivhan raised his voice, concern evident in his tone, as he addressed Anvit. "What drama are you doing? Have you been possessed by a ghost or something?" His words were filled with understanding, indicating that he wanted to grasp the reason behind Anvit's behavior and offer support.

Anvit's laughter continued as he responded, "No, no, I had a fight with my girlfriend today."

Then I asked, "If you're having conflicts with your girlfriend, what's the purpose of engaging in this dramatic behavior? Are you resorting to some form of occult practices or black magic?"

He gave me a thoughtful look and responded, "Hey Atharv, I think you've misunderstood. Let's sit down and have a conversation, and I'll explain my perspective." Anvit then proceeded to describe his approach to handling conflicts with his girlfriend. He emphasized the importance of understanding both sides of the argument by mentally placing himself in his girlfriend's shoes and vice versa. This approach allowed him to analyze the underlying reasons for the fight and seek potential solutions that would benefit both of them.

I was pleasantly surprised by Anvit's thoughtful and empathetic approach to resolving conflicts with his girlfriend. It showed his commitment to understanding and finding mutually beneficial resolutions.

He seemed to have a thoughtful and analytical perspective on the matter. I listened as he explained his process of examining the situation from both sides and then finding a solution that works for both of them. It was clear that he cared about his relationship and was willing to put in the effort to make it work. I told him that his approach was impressive and that I hoped to learn from his example.

He laughed and said that it was just his way of making things work and that everyone has their own methods. I said, "Yes, everyone has their own methods, but my girlfriend never gets angry with me nor does she get mad at me." Anvit said, "That's a good thing, it means you both understand each other." Then I said, "Yeah, I think so too.

Vivhan grew tired of our dialogue and scoffed at the idea that what we shared was true love. He believed it was nothing more than a fleeting attraction. He warned that when we inevitably face betrayal, we will look back and recall his prophetic words. And we both looked at him and said, 'You're a buzzkill. Go back and play basketball.

Vivhan left the room, making a derogatory remark about how girls always talk about such things. However, his comment only made us laugh harder at his childishness.

As soon as Vivhan left the room, I turned to Anvit and inquired about his girlfriend. I wanted to know if she was also studying engineering like us and how they met. Curiosity got the better of me, and I also asked Anvit what he thought of her.

Anvit shared that his girlfriend was two years older than him and lived in their neighborhood. She was pursuing a Bachelor of Commerce. When I confirmed with him if she was older than him, he laughed and confirmed that she was indeed older.

I was intrigued by Anvit's relationship with his girlfriend. It was apparent that he was very fond of her, and I could tell by the way he spoke about her that he cared deeply for her. I was also surprised to hear that she was older than him, as it was not a common scenario among our group of friends.

It was refreshing to see Anvit's different approach to relationships, as he seemed to value communication and compromise. I admired his maturity and level-headedness.

Anvit smiled and said that he was really lucky to have her in his life. He described her as kind, intelligent, and supportive. He went on to say that she always knows how to make him feel better when he is down and that he couldn't imagine his life without her.

I could see the love and admiration in Anvit's eyes as he spoke about his girlfriend. It was clear that he had a deep connection with her and valued her greatly. I felt happy for him and wished him all the best in his relationship.

As the days passed, our exam season drew closer, and the atmosphere in our dorm grew more and more tense. With each passing day, the pressure to perform well weighed heavily on everyone's minds. Late-night study sessions stressed conversations and restless nights became the norm as we dedicated ourselves to preparing for the upcoming exams. The anticipation and anxiety filled the air, making it palpable within the dormitory walls.

The students who were once determined to become the next Bill Gates or Mark Zuckerberg at the beginning of the session were now standing outside everyone's rooms, asking for help to pass their exams. This situation arose because some students struggled with understanding concepts and lacked knowledge, leading to the rise of a popular practice in college life known as "group study."

The purpose of group study was initially intended to create an environment where 3-4 students could gather and help one another by resolving doubts and clarifying concepts. However, the dynamic of group study underwent a change within the hostel students' approach. While they would initially come together to address their academic queries, it didn't take long for the atmosphere to shift. Instead of focusing solely on studying, they would eventually veer off into storytelling and engaging in casual conversations.

During our group study sessions, a recurring story that circulated among the students revolved around the chemistry lab, which had acquired a reputation for being haunted. According to popular belief, a malevolent ghost resided within the lab, ready to attack anyone who dared to enter. The rumors gained traction following a tragic incident in which a Ph.D. student lost their life in a lab accident.

As the tale unfolded, it was said that the vengeful ghost would seek retribution on anyone who entered the lab at night, inflicting them with a sinister demise. These chilling accounts contributed to an atmosphere of fear and apprehension surrounding the chemistry lab, captivating the imagination and giving rise to cautionary tales.

I laughed and expressed my disbelief, "That seems highly unlikely. What kind of story is that? Why would a ghost only appear in the lab at night and not during the day?" I then suggested, "Perhaps this story was created to discourage students from stealing chemicals by scaring them with the idea of a ghost at night." Vivhan agreed with my reasoning and added, "Atharv is absolutely right. There is no such thing as a ghost. These stories are all in our imagination."

As the other students remained skeptical about the ghost story, they proposed a bet to Vivhan and me. The terms of the wager were that if we didn't believe in the haunting, we would have to visit the lab at night. Intrigued by the challenge, I accepted without hesitation, stating confidently, "Yes, once the exams are over, we will certainly venture into the lab." Vivhan, sharing my determination, added, "Absolutely, count us in."

Upon the completion of the exams, a range of emotions swept through the student population. Some individuals expressed contentment with their performance, while others harbored a sense of dissatisfaction. However, regardless of their academic outcomes, a palpable sense of excitement permeated the hostel as everyone eagerly anticipated the forthcoming break.

Conversations filled the air as students enthusiastically discussed their plans for the break, whether it involved returning home to their families or embarking on adventures with friends. The hostel became a hub of animated chatter, buzzing with anticipation and the thrill of upcoming experiences.

Meanwhile, Vivhan and I had a different focus in mind. We eagerly looked forward to our planned nocturnal exploration of the chemistry lab, driven by a shared determination to dispel the pervasive myth of its haunting. With a keen desire to unravel the truth, we meticulously devised plans to meet the following week and commence our investigation.

After a week, Vivhan and I met up to carry out our investigation. We entered the lab and found everything in order. There was no sign of any ghost or paranormal activity. We roamed around the lab, examining the equipment and taking note of the various chemicals and substances stored there.

As we were about to leave, we heard a strange noise coming from one of the cabinets. It sounded like something was shuffling around inside. Our hearts raced with fear as we slowly approached the cabinet before I opened the door. Vivhan ran away from the lab and before leaving he closed the door. Mischievously, I blurted out 'Vivhan, you're such a cheat!

As I stood there in the silent lab, my heart pounding in my chest, my phone suddenly rang. I was surprised to see Aadhya's name flashing on the screen. How did she know I was in trouble? I hesitated for a moment, wondering whether or not to answer, but eventually picked up.

"Aadhya, where are you?" she asked me, her voice filled with concern.

"I'm in the lab," I replied, still feeling shaken by the eerie atmosphere.

"At night?" Aadhya sounded shocked. "What are you doing there?

Have you been there since morning?"

I quickly explained about the bet and why I was there. Aadhya's tone changed instantly. She was furious.

"Atharv, I've been waiting for your call since morning, and you're playing bets to go to the lab at night?" Her voice rose in anger. "You're so careless! You don't understand anything! Do you even remember what day it is today?"

I racked my brain, trying to remember if there was anything significant about the date. "No, what day is it?" I asked, feeling foolish.

"It's November 20th," Aadhya said, her voice breaking. "Atharv! And you didn't even remember! I've been waiting for your call all day, and you're here, playing bets at night!"

Her words pierced through me, and I felt a pang of guilt wash over me.

Aadhya's words hit me like a ton of bricks. How could I have forgotten our anniversary? I felt terrible. Aadhya continued to cry and scold me, and I knew that I had let her down. As I left the lab that night, As I realized the extent of my thoughtlessness, a sense of foolishness engulfed me. The realization that I had become so consumed by my own pursuits and neglected the person who held the utmost significance in my life left me with a deep sense of regret. Before I could even utter an apology, Aadhya abruptly ended the call. The abruptness of the disconnection hit me hard, intensifying the weight of my guilt. I was left alone with my thoughts, feeling terrible and burdened by the knowledge that my forgetfulness had caused her distress and upset.

As I stepped out of the lab, a wave of applause and cheers engulfed me from my friends and fellow students. They praised my supposed bravery for venturing into the haunted lab. However, beneath the facade of their admiration, a profound sadness consumed me. Inside, I felt like crumbling under the weight of Aadhya's scolding and the knowledge that I had let her down.

Amidst the external celebration, I couldn't escape the internal turmoil. A deep sorrow engulfed me as I grappled with the fact that this was the first time Aadhya had expressed such disappointment and frustration towards me. The thought that my actions had caused her pain tore at my heart, and I yearned for the chance to apologize and make things right.

Unfortunately, my attempts to reconcile were met with further obstacles. Aadhya had hung up the call before I could utter a sincere apology, and now her phone remained switched off, rendering any immediate communication impossible. The sense of helplessness intensified as I longed for the opportunity to express my remorse and seek forgiveness.

I was sitting alone in my thoughts when Anvit came up to me and broke the silence. "Why are you sitting so quietly?" he asked, his curious eyes fixated on me.

I hesitated for a moment before responding, trying to find a way to deflect the question. But he persisted, asking me again. Finally, I relented and told him about a phone call that had been weighing heavily on my mind. Anvit looked at me skeptically and asked, "Did you really forget about it, or are you just acting like you did?" I felt a pang of defensiveness rise within me. "Why would I lie about something like that?" I retorted.

But Anvit's response surprised me. "It's not about lying or telling the truth," he explained patiently. "Sometimes, we start acting before we even reveal our pain or mistakes. It's a way of gaining sympathy from the other person."

I paused for a moment, considering his words. "No, I'm not acting," I finally said. "In fact, I'm starting to feel how Aadhya must have been hurt because of me." My confession hung heavy in the air between us, and I felt a sense of relief at finally admitting the truth. As Anvit noticed tears welling up in my eyes, he placed a comforting hand on my shoulder and said, "Atharv, don't cry. It's okay." Then he asked, "Tell me more about Aadhya. Does she get upset over small things?"

Curious and intrigued by Anvit's unconventional approach, I shook my head and replied, "No, she doesn't even fight with me. This is the first time we had a fight like this."

Without further explanation, Anvit took a wooden stick and skillfully crafted two faces out of it—one with my name written on it and the other with Aadhya's name. He instructed me to speak to the face with my name on it first. Although initially unsure of the significance, I decided to give it a try, willing to explore this unique perspective.

As I spoke to the face representing myself, something unexpected happened. The act of addressing the face allowed me to verbalize my thoughts and emotions, providing a sense of clarity and self-reflection. It provided a platform for introspection, allowing me to articulate my feelings, concerns, and regrets without any external judgment.

However, it felt good and I looked at Anvit and said that it really works. Anvit laughed and said , "Actually, this trick works because it helps us see both sides of the situation and find a solution. It's a way of reminding ourselves that there are always multiple perspectives to consider."

Feeling a sense of clarity wash over me, I nodded in agreement. "You're right. I need to call Aadhya and talk to her."

Anvit grinned, patting me on the back. "That's the spirit! And don't worry, girls don't stay angry for too long. Call her and make up. Everything will be alright."

Feeling grateful for Anvit's guidance, I took out my phone and dialed Aadhya's number. As the phone rang, I couldn't help but feel nervous about what to say. But before I knew it, Aadhya picked up the phone and I heard her voice on the other end.Without wasting any time, I said to Aadhya, "You know how small the world is, and how few days we have in this small world. Even within those few days, we only get a handful of meaningful moments. If we spend those precious moments fighting with each other, do you think God will be pleased with us?"

As I tried to make amends, Aadhya scolded me for my forgetfulness and lack of ambition. "You should keep quiet," she said sharply. "First you forgot today's date, and now you're trying to trap me in your talks. Do you even know that I've been waiting for your call since morning, and you're just playing games?"

She continued, "I study here all day, while you're busy searching for ghosts over there, Atharv. I feel like you don't even love me, otherwise, you wouldn't be wasting your time like this. "Each syllable carried a weight of disappointment and longing, highlighting the emotional toll my actions had taken on her. The realization that my pursuits had made her question my love for her hit me hard, and a pang of guilt coursed through my veins.

Aadhya then recounted her parents' own struggles before they got married, highlighting the importance of hard work and dedication. "But with you, I cannot stay angry for too long because then who will take care of you?" she added, her tone softening.

You know that if you were caught in the lab at night, you could be expelled, and if you accidentally got hurt by acid, you didn't even think about that. You could have at least thought about me."

Feeling ashamed, I promised her that I wouldn't make the same mistake again. But Aadhya wasn't convinced. "No, Atharv, if I let you go like this, you might make the same mistake again. I need you to understand the gravity of the situation," she said sternly.

I pleaded with her not to cut off contact with me, but she insisted that I needed to learn from my mistake. "I won't talk to you for a week," she declared, her tone final. "Maybe then you'll realize the severity of your actions."

Desperately, I requested her not to hang up, but it was too late. Aadhya had already ended the call, leaving me to contemplate my foolishness and the consequences of my actions.

"After listening to so much scolding, I understood how she used to win the debate competitions because no one could speak in front of her. She scolded so much in one breath that I still needed time to understand those things."I was in a solemn mood when there was a fight going on between two boys in our hostel corridor.

Since it was a hostel fight, students from every block were coming to see it, and everyone was cheering."

It seemed as if everyone wanted to enjoy this fight. When I asked why those two boys were fighting, some boys didn't know the reason. In fact, they asked me to enjoy the moment, even though I didn't like to watch fights. But still, to know the reason, I was standing there and asking. One of the boys then told me that there was a fight going on between Dhoni and Gambhir supporters over who played better in the World Cup match.I started laughing at the reason for their fight, and then Aadhya called me.

I chuckled and greeted her with a laugh, "Hello." Aadhya inquired about my current activity, and I responded, "Just witnessing a scuffle here." Aadhya sighed and replied, "Oh Atharv, what am I going to do with you?" before ending the call. And at that moment, I found myself pondering, "What could possibly be my fault now?"

And then a message popped up that said, "It's been two weeks now, don't talk to me.

I was just thinking about how strange this was happening to me and what kind of form this goddess has taken after I came to college. With a mind brimming with confusion, I resolved to seek the guidance of a senior in my college. I had a burning question in my mind regarding placements and the salary packages offered by the college.

But what caught my attention was when they advised me to enhance my coding skills and contribute to open-source projects. They explained that this would increase my chances of getting a better package. They even suggested some books and gave me guidance on how to improve my skills.

Moreover, they warned me that no one in the college would tell me about the projects they were working on or the internships they were taking. So, it was crucial to be prepared for all these things beforehand. After expressing my gratitude, I decided to take their advice and started working towards honing my coding skills.

As I started following the advice of my senior, I began to focus more on my studies. Between attending lectures, and labs, and working on coding questions, I didn't have much time to hang out with the other hostel mates. Consequently, I found it challenging to initiate conversations with them, and once again, I felt lonely in the midst of a crowd.

While engrossed in my work, my phone suddenly rang, shattering my concentration. I noticed that it was Aadhya calling. She questioned if I had forgotten about her since she had requested a two-week break from talking, but it had already been three weeks since our last conversation.

Surprised, I informed her that I had been overwhelmed with work and hadn't had a chance to catch up. I elaborated on my hectic schedule, and she sympathized with me. Then, she revealed that she would be visiting her aunt in Delhi tomorrow. To my astonishment, she extended an invitation for me to come and meet her at her aunt's place. Filled with excitement, I eagerly replied, "Yes, yes, I will come!"

The following day, filled with anticipation, I reached out to my friend Anvit, requesting to borrow his Nike shoes for the day. He graciously agreed, understanding my eagerness to make a good impression. Additionally, I approached a senior, seeking their assistance in lending me their bike for the occasion. Thankfully, they kindly obliged, recognizing the importance of this meeting for me.

As I arrived at Aadhya's aunt's place, my heart raced with a mix of excitement and nervousness. A sense of relief washed over me as her aunt opened the door, wearing a warm smile. With a friendly tone, she inquired if I was Atharv, verifying my identity. Affirming my name, I greeted her with a smile and expressed my gratitude for the invitation. Appreciating her hospitality, she graciously invited me inside, setting the stage for what promised to be a memorable encounter.

Aadhya's aunt proved to be a kind-hearted woman, embodying warmth and hospitality. As I stepped inside, she kindly offered me a refreshing glass of water and gestured for me to take a seat. Appreciating her thoughtfulness, I gratefully accepted the drink, quenching my thirst.

Curiosity brimming within me, I couldn't help but inquire about Aadhya's whereabouts. To my delight, her aunt informed me that she was busy in the kitchen, preparing my favorite dish, Rajma Chawal, especially for me. A surge of joy and gratitude swept through me at the news. It was a delightful surprise to know that Aadhya had taken such care to make my visit special.

At that moment, I realized how fortunate I was to be in the presence of such a considerate host.

As I stepped into the kitchen, the enticing aroma of the food engulfed my senses, drawing me closer to where the culinary magic was taking place. Aadhya, donning an apron, stood by the stove, a radiant smile gracing her face. Mesmerized by her beauty, I couldn't help but admire her even more as she skillfully prepared the meal.

Filled with excitement and curiosity, I couldn't resist expressing my surprise, "Aadhya, you're making Rajma Chawal for me?" The words escaped my lips, laced with a mix of astonishment and delight. Aadhya turned towards me, a sparkle in her eyes, and responded with a hint of playful reproach, "Well, I scolded you so much that I thought you had forgotten about me."

Her words were accompanied by a gentle chuckle, making it clear that her playful comment was in good humor.

With a lightness in her tone, Aadhya revealed the intention behind her culinary endeavor. She expressed her desire to persuade me to come and indulge in my favorite dish, acknowledging that her version might not match the taste of my mother's preparation. A hint of playfulness laced her words as she added, "So if it's not tasty, you can still eat it." Her laughter echoed in the kitchen

Then, Aadhya's aunt came into the kitchen and told Aadhya that she could now talk to me and that she would take care of the rest of the cooking.

Aadhya's smile remained on her face as she turned towards me. With a gentle suggestion, she proposed, "Let's sit outside." Following her lead, we stepped out of the kitchen, moving towards a more relaxed setting. However, to my surprise, as soon as we exited the kitchen, she suddenly slapped me, catching me off guard. Her words followed swiftly, "This is because you didn't call me."

Shocked momentarily, I couldn't help but burst into laughter, realizing the playfulness behind her action. In that instant, I embraced her in a warm hug, expressing my genuine joy at seeing her. Amidst our laughter and embrace, I responded, "You have no idea how happy I am to see you."

Aadhya, still within the realm of jest, shared her reason for coming, saying, "I just came to make sure that my Atharv hasn't gone astray in the Delhi air." Her words evoked a smile. With a lighthearted response, the conversation shifted, and I eagerly asked her about her college life, eager to hear her experiences and share in the journey that shaped her.

As Aadhya began to share the details of her hectic schedule, I listened attentively, fully aware of the challenges she faced in managing her time and commitments. Her words painted a vivid picture of the demands placed upon her, highlighting the numerous responsibilities she had to juggle.

With empathy in my voice, I expressed my understanding, acknowledging the weight of her busy routine. I reassured her that I recognized the effort she put into her studies and other engagements, and I admired her determination to excel in all aspects of her college life.

Seeking to alleviate some of her stress, I asked if there was any way I could support her or assist her in finding a balance. I wanted her to know that she didn't have to face the challenges alone and that I was there to lend a helping hand whenever she needed it.

Aadhya's smile brightened the room as she expressed her gratitude, saying, "Oh, Atharv, thank youuuuu." Her appreciation filled me with warmth, knowing that my words had resonated with her.

Shortly after, Aadhya's aunt called us for lunch, and we eagerly gathered around the table. We sat down at the table and started eating. The food was delicious, and I could tell that Aadhya had put in a lot of effort to make it perfect for me.

Aadhya's aunt inquired if I was naturally a shy person or if there was a particular topic that made me feel embarrassed. To this, Aadhya intervened and said, "No, Aunty, Atharv is always like this. He tends to be shy just like a girl when it comes to such matters. "Then, Aadhya's aunt started laughing and as we finished our lunch she asked Aadhya to take the dishes to the kitchen.

As soon as Aadhya left with the dishes, Aadhya's aunt turned to me and said, "You won't betray my daughter, will you?" I was taken aback and replied, "No, aunty, why would I do that?" Aadhya's aunt then said, "Okay, good. She's my only niece, and I care about her a lot. If you hurt her, I will personally make sure you go to jail." I was speechless and just nodded my head in agreement.And then she laughed and said, "I'm just kidding.

You're such a cute boy." After expressing her concern, she added, "But please refrain from causing any harm to my daughter." To assure her, I responded respectfully, "Certainly, Aunty, you need not worry. I will ensure her safety. If you don't mind, may I take Aadhya for a walk?" Understanding my request,

Aunty replied, "Yes, you may, but kindly ensure that you bring her back within an hour."

As Aadhya and I arrived at a nearby park, we decided to indulge in some ice cream before strolling around. While walking, I took the opportunity to inquire about her happiness, asking, "Are you enjoying yourself, Aadhya?" Curious about my earlier statement, she questioned, "Yes, I am happy, but why did you say that?" I casually replied, "Just thought it would be nice to hear your thoughts."

In response, Aadhya revealed, "Sometimes, I simply miss your captivating stories." Sensing her nostalgia, I offered, "Well, if you ever feel like hearing one, just let me know." However, she gently declined, saying, "No, let me cherish this moment, so that the upcoming semesters won't make me miss you too much."

In that moment, a bittersweet silence enveloped us, as if neither of us wanted to bid farewell to one another. Suddenly, Aadhya's aunt called, indicating that it was time for her to return home. Aadhya swiftly responded, assuring her aunt that she would be home within just five minutes.

As our eyes met, Aadhya spoke softly, "Turn your face, please.

As I turned to face her, Aadhya's voice resonated with sincerity and vulnerability. She expressed, "Atharv, I trust you so much. Please don't ever break my trust." I could sense the genuine concern in her words. She continued, "I was just a little scared, which is why I scolded you. If you ever feel like I'm being too controlling, just tell me, but please don't leave me."

Her heartfelt plea touched my heart deeply. A wave of warmth and affection washed over me as I looked into her adorable face, reminiscent of a dewdrop delicately resting on a leaf in the morning. I reassured her with utmost sincerity, "Aadhya, I cherish the trust you have in me, and I promise to honor it always.

With a smile of reassurance, I proceeded to drop Aadhya off at her aunt's house.

As I was walking towards the hostel, my mind was filled with thoughts of the girl I once wanted to talk to, see, and know the name of. And now, I realized that she was afraid of losing me today. It felt like God had blessed me with all the happiness in the world, and it seemed like all my dreams had come true.

However, as we all know, days can be long but years are short, and these college days were passing by quickly. Even though we were busy organizing festivals and enjoying our college life, we never compromised on our studies. We understood the value of education and the importance of academic excellence. We managed our time effectively, balancing our social activities with our studies. We were committed to achieving our academic goals while also making the most of our college experiences.

But there was an incident in college that completely changed my perspective. This incident happened in the girls' hostel, where a girl had committed suicide.

Later, it was revealed that her own roommate had created a fake Facebook profile in her name, through which she engaged in inappropriate conversations with boys from college. The poor girl's reputation was tarnished due to the fake profile, and when she realized it, she took the extreme step of ending her life .After this incident, I was shocked and hurt to think that one girl could do such a thing to another girl.

The culture I come from places a strong emphasis on respect for girls, and women are revered as goddesses. It was quite challenging for me to comprehend how one girl could stoop so low as to bring down another girl and engage in such a heinous act. This incident opened my eyes to the fact that not all girls embody the virtuous qualities often associated with the goddess Sita; some may also have shades of Surpanakha.

This realization forced me to confront the complexity of human nature. It made me understand that individuals, regardless of their gender, possess a range of characteristics and are capable of both positive and negative actions. Just as there are women who exemplify grace, kindness, and integrity, there are also those who may display traits that are less desirable.

Now, no one can truly fathom the depth of potential within that girl or comprehend the loneliness she must have experienced in her life, unable to confide her thoughts with anyone. When I shared this incident with Aadhya, even she was taken aback, questioning why people resort to defaming others. It was during this conversation that I expressed to Aadhya that regardless of how negatively Shreya may speak about me, at least she remains loyal to her friend. I respected her for that.

Aadhya clarified that Shreya doesn't speak ill of me; she simply doesn't want to witness her friend in a vulnerable or hurt state.

And then I recalled the words of Shantanu, who advised me to stay away from Aadhya. It made me contemplate the similarity between Shreya and Shantanu, as both of them shared the common desire of safeguarding their friend from any harm. This realization made me think that their intentions were aligned, despite any differences they might have had.

Furthermore, as I reflected on the portrayal of love in movies and web series, it became apparent to me how society has increasingly focused on the physical aspects of love. This narrow representation has led to a lack of understanding when it comes to the true essence of relationships and love. People struggle to grasp the deeper meaning and emotional connection that should accompany love, often equating it solely with physical attraction. This societal influence has contributed to confusion and misunderstanding among individuals seeking genuine relationships.

6

Ending?

I called Iti after two hours, but she didn't pick up the call. I tried calling again, and this time she answered. She told me that she would talk to me later, but I insisted that she tell me how Aadhya was doing. Iti then informed me that Aadhya had a fever and was not feeling well.

I (Sandhya) asked Atharv with a mixture of surprise and curiosity, "Where did this story suddenly come from?" My emotions were evident as I was taken aback by Iti's sudden appearance and the unexpected revelation of this story.

And then, my parents entered the room, causing a momentary pause in the conversation. My father spoke up, his voice carrying a sense of urgency, "Atharv, we received a call from your home. Your father informed us that your flight is scheduled soon, and you should make your way back home without any further delay."

I pleaded, "Just give us two more minutes, Dad," while my father, a mix of curiosity and impatience, glanced at his watch. A look of surprise crossed his face as he realized, "It's already been two hours." As my mother prepared to leave, she expressed a mix of amusement and bewilderment, saying, "The new generation these days, never stop talking about their relationships." A touch of nostalgia tinted her words as she added, "In our time, we used to feel embarrassed just talking about it." The atmosphere lightened with laughter.

Atharv expressed his apologies, realizing that he had gotten carried away while narrating the story. He acknowledged the time constraint, saying, "Sorry, Sandhya. I got lost somewhere while narrating the story, but now, I'm running late. Can I continue the rest of the story in our next meeting?"

Understanding the situation, I nodded and replied, "Yes, that's perfectly fine. We can continue the story in our next meeting." We both agreed to resume the conversation at a later time, allowing Atharv to attend to his pressing matters and ensuring we could delve deeper into the story at a more suitable opportunity.

However, before concluding our discussion, I felt compelled to ask Atharv one thing. In response, Atharv looked at me with his charming expression, indicating his willingness to answer my question. He responded, "Yes, go ahead and ask."

With a mix of confusion and concern, I directly addressed Atharv, expressing my doubts and seeking clarity. I asked, "You mentioned that Aadhya was the girl who played a significant role in your success. However, I fail to comprehend why, if you both loved each other deeply, you find yourself here today. You are aware of the reason my parents called you for our marriage, aren't you? And if you were aware of it, why did you choose to share this story with me? Because now, knowing about your past relationship, I might even consider refusing to proceed with our marriage."

Atharv took a moment to absorb the weight of my words, understanding the implications of my concerns. He then responded, "Yes, I acknowledge that you may now be inclined to refuse me based on this revelation. However, I urge you to consider this perspective: What if I were to conceal my past until after our marriage? Wouldn't that be unfair and potentially lead to even greater complications and misunderstandings down the line?"

His words highlighted the importance of openness and trust in a relationship, suggesting that sharing his past with me beforehand was a way to establish a foundation of honesty and avoid future complications. The decision, ultimately, lay in my hands, and Atharv awaited my response with a mix of apprehension and hope.

With a thoughtful expression, Atharv continued, "I am well aware of the reason your parents have invited me here. They want us to consider marriage. That's precisely why I decided to share my past with you. I believe that for us to make an informed decision about spending our lives together, it is crucial for you to have clarity and a deeper understanding of who I am. After all, deciding to commit to someone based on a mere two-hour meeting can be a challenging task."

Atharv took a moment to gather his thoughts, and then he added, "I thought it would be better to initiate our journey by sharing my story, as it would provide you with valuable insights into my life and experiences. It's an opportunity for you to understand me better and make a more informed decision about whether we should proceed with this union."

His words hung in the air, inviting contemplation and reflection, as we both recognized the importance of transparency and open communication in building a strong foundation for our potential relationship.

With a cautious tone, I mustered the courage to ask, "Did she, perchance, betray your trust?" My voice carried a mix of concern and curiosity, aware that delving into such sensitive territory could unravel hidden emotions.

Atharv responded with a heartfelt conviction, "Love is not something that can be reduced to the concept of cheating when it is not reciprocated. Love transcends such boundaries. It is an emotion that defies categorization, where notions of breakups and betrayal hold no relevance. Love is about surrender, just like a priest's devotion to his God, a peacock's love for the rain clouds, or a river's journey to the ocean. When your love reaches an extreme level, it becomes respect, and there are no questions about it.

"I then asked, 'Is the meaning of this that those who are in love should not necessarily act on it? Because neither can all priests see God, nor do all rivers get the ocean, nor does it always rain for the peacock.'"

"Atharv laughed heartily and said, 'Neither do we live for any eternity, so should we stop living just because we will all die someday?' I chuckled in agreement and replied, 'No.'

Atharv, while trying to convey his understanding, said, "Love is not about saying, 'Because I love you, now you have to be mine.' Love is more like saying, 'Because I love you, now I am yours.' It's about selflessness and surrendering oneself to the other person."

He continued, "The feeling of worship is incredibly significant, even more so than merely seeing God. In any religion, those who have experienced the presence of God cannot fully describe Him, yet we acknowledge His existence. The act of patiently waiting for rain clouds, as the peacock does, is a profound expression of love. It encompasses elements of patience, faith, and devotion. The peacock demonstrates its unwavering commitment by waiting for an uncertain amount of time for the arrival of the rain clouds."

"The journey of a river meeting the ocean is another example of love. In this union, the river loses its own identity for the sake of the vastness and unity of the ocean," Atharv added.

"These experiences cannot be fully explained or comprehended; they can only be felt and lived. Love goes beyond mere explanations or understanding. It is a deep emotional connection that surpasses words and actions. It is the feeling of being connected to someone or something that is greater than ourselves, and it is this feeling that gives life its deepest meaning and purpose.

"My mother called out, 'Atharv, the cab has arrived and Sandhya, will you please let him go?' I then interjected, 'Sorry, you should leave now, or else my mom will kill me. But remember, you have to come back and tell me the rest of the story.'" Atharv nodded in agreement.

We descended the stairs together, making our way down. My mother gave me a stern look, emphasizing that Atharv was running out of time. Just as Atharv was about to step into the cab, I exclaimed, "Wait a second!" and hurriedly rushed towards the kitchen. My father playfully commented, "This girl will only be happy if she makes him late."

Returning with a bowl of curd and rock sugar in my hand, I approached Atharv. Requesting him to open his mouth, I explained, "Whenever we embark on an auspicious endeavor, we consume curd and sugar to symbolize the sweetness we wish to add to our lives."

Atharv smiled warmly, willingly accepting the curd and mishri, and expressed his gratitude before finally departing.

My mom asked me, her voice tinged with a blend of curiosity, concern, and surprise, "Has he become so incredibly likable to you that you didn't want to let him go? Initially, you even adamantly refused to meet him. What kind of inexplicable magic has he worked upon you?" Her eyebrows furrowed slightly, reflecting her genuine puzzlement and desire to understand the depth of my emotions.

I replied, "No, it's not like that. I just thought that we should treat our guests well, that's all." I shrugged, trying to downplay the situation. Then, I quickly made my way to my room, feeling a mix of relief and a desire to retreat to my personal space.

Atharv, who is the son of my dad's friend, was someone I had been avoiding meeting for the past six months. My dad had been persuading me to meet him, but I kept finding excuses because I wasn't ready for marriage and had no such plans. However, today, due to my parent's insistence, I finally agreed to meet him. I had thought that I would simply decline after meeting him.

However, things didn't go as I had planned. When I saw Atharv, his simplicity, and appearance gave off positive vibes. His face radiated a calmness like that of a moon, which brought a sense of peace to my eyes.

In his hands, he held a red religious thread, without any fancy smartwatch, bracelet, or ring. When he spoke to me, I noticed that he had put his phone on silent mode. He had an untamed beard, yet his hair was well-combed, adding to his overall charm.

As I was bringing tea, he stood up and took the tray from me. He gestured for me to sit down first, showing his consideration and politeness. When my parents left us alone, he first asked if I was comfortable and ready to talk. His thoughtfulness made me feel at ease and appreciated.

Both of us remained silent; it's not that I am a shy girl, but the atmosphere felt a bit awkward because I had forgotten the script of what I wanted to say.

So, Atharv took the initiative and started the conversation. He asked if I also read novels, perhaps noticing a book that I had left behind. I replied with a "yes," but my voice sounded exactly like I was pretending to be someone else as if I was acting to impress him. Now, in hindsight, I can't help but laugh at myself and wonder what had come over me.

Then, I told Atharv that he could ask me any questions he wanted. He chuckled and responded that he didn't come here to conduct an interview; in fact, his dad had simply asked him to meet a friend's daughter. I laughed as well and said, "Yeah, even my dad has been after me to meet Atharv."

At that moment, I mustered up the courage to speak openly and said, "I mean, you're here to meet me because of your father too, right?" Atharv nodded, his smile widening, and replied, "Yes, that's true." We shared a mutual understanding and found solace in the fact that our fathers had played a role in bringing us together.

As our conversation progressed, time seemed to slip away unnoticed. It felt as if we had just sat down and started talking, yet it seemed like hours had passed. The connection and chemistry between us were palpable, and it felt as if we had known each other for much longer than we actually had. The ease of our interaction made it feel like we had only just begun our conversation, despite the passage of time.

When he shared his past with me, instead of feeling any negative emotions, I felt a genuine understanding and empathy toward him. His vulnerability only deepened my appreciation for his honesty. Yet, despite having a valid reason to reject him, I couldn't help but find myself contemplating his presence in my life.

As he narrated his story, it felt as if he was still living in those moments. Every detail of his tale was etched in his memory, making it feel like a recent conversation. In a time where friends often ignore or block each other after a while, he stood out as someone who cherished the memories of his departed friend. It was as if he held onto them like precious currency, safeguarding them within himself. It was a testament to his loyalty, compassion, and the depth of his emotions.

Listening to him, it seemed as if he didn't worry about creating a favorable image or putting up a facade. He openly shared his mistakes and emotions, without any pretense. It was evident that he didn't care about hiding his vulnerabilities and flaws. In fact, his genuine and transparent approach made me feel as if he was being his authentic self, without any pretense or masks.

Moreover, some aspects of his storytelling made it seem like he was a "mama's boy," someone who cherished his relationship with his mother and held it in high regard. This perception arose from the way he spoke about certain things, which reflected a deep sense of love and respect for his mother. It added another layer to his character and made him even more intriguing.

The aspect that attracted me the most was his way of describing love. In a time when people often resort to abusing their ex-partners and trying to ruin their lives, he stood out as someone who had completely transformed the language of love. He showed me a different perspective, one that emphasized respect, understanding, and genuine care for the person he loved.

His words and sentiments resonated deeply with me, as he spoke of love as a pure and selfless connection. It was refreshing to encounter someone who believed in nurturing and uplifting their loved ones, rather than tearing them down. His perspective on love changed my perception and ignited a sense of hope and faith in the power of genuine affection.

The mention of Shantanu seemed to bring a hint of sadness to Atharv's eyes as if he still carried some emotional weight related to that name. However, when he spoke about Aadhya, his face lit up with a radiant glow. These contrasting reactions did raise some doubts and questions in my mind. It made me wonder about the nature of Atharv's connection with Shantanu and the depth of his feelings for Aadhya.

Perhaps there were unresolved emotions or a complicated history associated with Shantanu, which caused a touch of sorrow to resurface. On the other hand, the mention of Aadhya seemed to evoke joy and excitement, suggesting a strong positive bond between them. These observations made me curious to delve deeper into Atharv's experiences and understand the dynamics of his relationships.

It's possible that the loss of Shantanu was unpredictable or left a significant impact on Atharv's life, while the separation from

Aadhya might have been a mutual decision or involved additional circumstances.

As my parents entered the room, my father asked me how I found the boy. I replied, "Dad, why did you choose this boy? Just because he is your friend's son?"

Pausing for a moment, my father considered his words before responding, "Perhaps, yes. Maybe it's because I have known Atharv and his family for a long time."

"But Dad, I understand that you have a wide network of acquaintances, but what makes Atharv so special? He mentioned when Atharv's father faced a financial crisis and his business went bankrupt, he didn't resort to laying off his employees.

Instead, he made a selfless decision to mortgage his own house in order to save the factory and protect their livelihoods. Atharv's mother even made sacrifices by selling her jewelry during that challenging period. It's remarkable to think that all of this happened when Atharv was just around 3 years old. Such acts of kindness and sacrifice are truly exceptional."

My father patiently explained, "I thought it would be valuable for you to meet Atharv because his parents have demonstrated exceptional qualities of kindness and selflessness. It's highly likely that Atharv has been raised in an environment that fosters these same values. By getting to know him, you might discover a person with similar qualities who could positively influence your life as well."

Surprised, I exclaimed, "Oh, so that's the reason. But how does that relate to our marriage? I'm feeling really confused, Dad."

My dad smiled and replied, "Sandhya, when you want to assess someone's character, observe how they handle difficult times. Liking Atharv doesn't mean you have to marry him. simply wanted you to meet him, get to know him, and then make your decision. In fact, if there's someone else you like, you can tell me. I have no problem with that either."

I said, "No, Dad, I don't like any other guy. I'm just thinking that everything shouldn't rush into place all of a sudden.

And to be honest, I don't want to leave you and Mom.

My dad chuckled and said, "All right, whatever you wish."

It brought a smile to my face, knowing that my dad understood my hesitation.

My dad left the room, giving me some privacy. I could sense that he wanted my mom to be there for me, to understand the feelings in my heart.

My mom looked at me and asked, "Did you offer him curd and mishri before getting to know him? Was he a guest or did you actually like him?" I blushed and replied, "Mom, if you're going to talk about that, then you also leave the room. I feel embarrassed, I don't know why I did that."

My mom understood my embarrassment and shared a smile with me. She said, "Okay, dear. I'll leave you alone. Take your time and think things through. Remember, we're always here for you."

I held her back, stopping her from going any further. Overwhelmed with emotions, I sought solace in my mother's warm embrace. Resting my head on her shoulder, I mustered the courage to ask her the question that had been weighing heavily on my heart. How could I determine whether Atharv was the right person for me or not? It was a decision of immense significance, and I needed guidance from the person I trusted the most.

My mother gently caressed my back and spoke with a soothing tone. She said, "My dear, making such decisions is never easy, and there is no foolproof formula for knowing if someone is right for you. It requires careful thought, self-reflection, and listening to your heart."

She continued, "Start by considering the qualities and values that are important to you in a life partner. Think about your compatibility, shared goals, and aspirations. "Remember, no one is perfect, and every relationship requires effort and compromise.

Think about whether you can see a future with Atharv, where you support and uplift each other. Take your time, and don't rush into any decision."

She paused, giving me a moment to absorb her words. Then she added, "Talk to Atharv openly and honestly about your thoughts, feelings, and concerns. Communication is key in any relationship. And remember, we are here to support you no matter what choice you make. Trust yourself, my dear, and follow your heart."

I inquired about her impression of Dad, and she responded with a light-hearted chuckle, revealing that she hadn't even seen him before. However, she shared her unwavering trust in her own father and her belief that whatever she would receive would be good. With a touch of gratitude, she expressed her feelings of luck, as I already knew. Her words carried a sense of contentment and a reflection on the positive outcome that her faith had brought into her life.

I smiled in response and, acknowledged her perspective. With a sense of resolution, I stated, "Okay, I will take some time to think and make a decision. I will let you know, Mom." After expressing my intentions, my mom left the room, leaving me with my thoughts and the weight of the decision ahead.

I have formulated a plan to refuse someone in the morning, but at this moment, I am contemplating whether I should communicate this decision to them or keep it to myself. Should I initiate a phone call or should I exercise patience and wait?

Should I confide in my friend and share these thoughts or should I postpone discussing it for the time being? The sheer amount of confusion I am experiencing is overwhelming, and I find it difficult to comprehend and make sense of it all.

On one side, I feel a sense of shame just by contemplating the situation, while on the other side, I question the timing and necessity of taking action now. If not now, then when would be the appropriate time for me to embark on the journey of marriage? I feel like I might be overthinking things.

Perhaps I will ask the person who initiated this confusion during our next meeting.

Atharv's observation that around 80% of our thoughts tend to be negative was indeed accurate. Even after he shared his personal story with me, I still find myself questioning his transparency. Perhaps this doubt arises because trust is not easily given in the kind of society we live in.

It can indeed be challenging to have trust in the concept of love, given the prevalence of negativity and deception in today's world. In fact, I have come across instances where people discourage others from believing in love and instead suggest seeking someone else. This makes it even more difficult to maintain faith in love stories like that of Atharv's.

Numerous doubts have started to emerge in my mind. For instance, if he had feelings for Aadhya before, will he have the same level of affection for me? Will he genuinely understand me? Moreover, why did he keep the real reason for their separation hidden?

Could it be because he doesn't want to commit to marriage? Should I consider meeting Aadhya as well to uncover the true cause behind their story?

The way Atharv described Aadhya to me is making me feel jealous just thinking about her. I wonder what will happen when I meet her.

The most significant question in all of this is, if our positions were reversed and I were in Atharv's shoes, would he be as accepting of my past as I would be of his?

I hope that in our next meeting, I will find the answers to all these questions.

Now my eyes are feeling tired. All right, "Secret Keeper" (diary name). We will discuss this matter further. Until then, I bid you farewell.